My
SPARKLING
FAIRIES
Collection

ORCHARD BOOKS

Original editions of *Destiny, Flora, Florence, Belle, Selena, Shannon, Keira* and *Holly* first published
in Great Britain in 2009, 2007, 2011, 2010, 2011, 2008, 2012 and 2004 respectively by Orchard Books

Early Reader editions of each first published in 2014, 2012, 2012,
2013, 2014, 2013, 2015 and 2017 respectively by Orchard Books

This treasury containing Early Reader text and artwork first published in 2016 by The Watts Publishing Group
This edition published in 2017 by The Watts Publishing Group

3 5 7 9 10 8 6 4

A CIP catalogue record for this book is available from the British Library.

ISBN 978 1 40834 262 6

Printed and bound in China

MIX
Paper from
responsible sources
FSC® C104740

The paper and board used in this book are made from wood from responsible sources

Orchard Books
An imprint of Hachette Children's Group
Part of The Watts Publishing Group Limited
Carmelite House
50 Victoria Embankment
London EC4Y 0DZ

An Hachette UK Company
www.hachette.co.uk
www.hachettechildrens.co.uk

RAINBOW magic

My SPARKLING FAIRIES Collection

www.rainbowmagic.co.uk

Contents

Destiny the Pop Star Fairy   6

Flora the Fancy Dress Fairy   48

Florence the Friendship Fairy   90

Belle the Birthday Fairy   134

Selena the Sleepover Fairy   176

Shannon the Ocean Fairy   220

Keira the Film Star Fairy   264

Holly the Christmas Fairy   306

Destiny the Pop Star Fairy

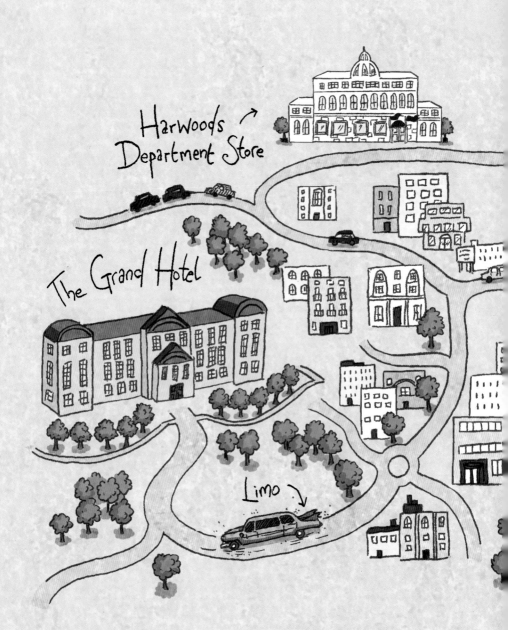

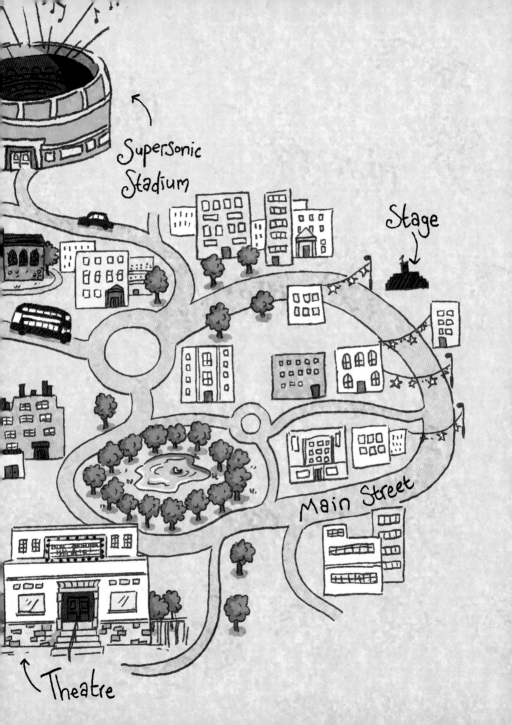

The Sparkle Sash

"I can't believe we're really going to meet Serena, Emilia and Lexy!" said Kirsty Tate to her best friend Rachel Walker. The girls had won a competition to meet their favourite band, The Angels.

The girls were staying overnight with their parents at The Grand Hotel before helping the band turn on the city's Christmas lights, and attending a charity concert. "This is almost as exciting as one of our fairy adventures!" Rachel whispered to her best friend. No one else knew that they had a special friendship with the fairies.

"Oh, Rachel, look!" cried Kirsty. On a table in a corner of their room was a huge bunch of flowers, with a handwritten card on top. It was from the girls in the band!

Dear Kirsty and Rachel,
We hope you have a fun stay! We are really looking forward to meeting you later today. Serena, Emilia & Lexy
— The Angels xxx

"Look at the Christmas tree!" cried Rachel, as they explored their enormous suite. As she spoke, there was a burst of glitter, and a beautiful fairy appeared.

"Hello," she began in a tinkling voice. "I'm Destiny the Pop Star Fairy, and I need your help."

The delighted but startled girls waited for her to explain.

"I look after pop stars in the human world and Fairyland," she began. "Jack Frost wants to perform at our Christmas concert, but his group's audition was awful!

Now he's so cross he says he'll rid the world of pop music completely!"

"How could Jack Frost get rid of all music?" asked a horrified Kirsty.

"I have three magical objects," sighed the tiny fairy. "The Sparkle Sash protects pop stars' outfits and costumes. The Keepsake Key protects their songs and music, and the Magical Microphone ensures the sound and lighting work smoothly." The girls listened as Destiny continued.

"Jack Frost has stolen them, and ordered his goblins to hide them. He wants to spoil The Angels' Christmas concert at the same time."

"But that's tomorrow!" gasped Kirsty. "What can we do to help?"

"Stay alert," said Destiny. "The goblins are bound to cause trouble sooner or later."

It was time for the girls to head for the stadium, and all thoughts of Jack Frost and goblins flew from their minds. They were about to meet The Angels! Arriving at the stage door,

the girls were led to the band's dressing room. The door opened, and The Angels rushed over. "Congratulations on winning the competition!" Serena said with a smile.

"It's great to meet you!" Lexy added, her copper-coloured ringlets bouncing.

"You're going to get star treatment from our own stylists," Emilia told them. "But first we're going to teach you the dance routine for our brand-new song!"

Rachel and Kirsty were giggling with The Angels like old friends as the door opened. "Girls, meet Rich and Charlotte, our stylist and make-up artist," said Emilia. As Charlotte dabbed glitter onto their cheeks and eyelids, and Rich talked about what clothes would suit them, Emilia's mobile phone began to ring. Her face fell as soon as she answered it. "But this could ruin the whole show!" she cried. Rachel and Kirsty exchanged worried looks. Could this have something to do with Jack Frost? Emilia ended the call.

"The lorry carrying our costumes hasn't turned up!" she explained.

As everyone began talking at once, the girls slipped into the corridor. A little way down, a storage room door was open.

"Oh, no!" said Kirsty, stepping inside.

The room was a mess. Shimmering costumes were smeared with purples, blues and golds and someone had used red lipstick to draw a picture of Jack Frost on the wall!

"Goblins!" muttered Kirsty crossly.

Suddenly a jet of glitter shot from the top of a silver boot, and Destiny appeared.

"We must find the Sparkle Sash before the goblins cause any more trouble!" she said, waving her wand and clearing the room in a flurry of magical sparkles.

The friends followed a horrible screeching sound to the stage, where the goblins were all dressed up and trying to sing.

"Look!" Kirsty exclaimed, pointing to something shimmery tied around the smallest goblin's waist.

"It's the Sparkle Sash!" Destiny exclaimed. "But how can we get it?"

"Let's teach them The Angels' dance routine!" smiled Kirsty. "Then you take the sash!"

Amid the chaos of clumsily dancing goblins, Destiny managed to untie the sash. She returned it to fairy size, and flitted away.

"Carry on practising!" Kirsty called out, running off the stage.

"They've stolen my sash!" shrieked the goblin furiously.

The disappointed goblins shuffled off towards the exit as Destiny waved her wand to clear up the stage. "Thank you so much for your help, girls," she said. "I could never have got this back without you."

"Are you going to take the sash back to Fairyland now?" asked Kirsty.

Destiny nodded.

"The sooner it's back in its rightful place, the better!" she declared.

Rachel and Kirsty waved as Destiny disappeared in a whirl of sparkles. "Come on," whispered Rachel. "Let's get back to The Angels!"

In the dressing room, Rachel and Kirsty found The Angels hugging and jumping around in excitement. "The lorry has been found!" Lexy squealed happily. "The driver's satnav sent him the wrong way, then the lorry broke down, then his mobile battery ran out. But just then a breakdown truck rescued him, and his satnav started working again. Can you believe it?"

"It's amazing the truck was found so quickly,

and then found its way here!" said Serena to the two friends.

"It's like magic!" agreed Kirsty, winking at Rachel.

Now there were only two more magical objects left to find!

The Keepsake Key

Next morning, Mr Tate had a surprise for the girls. "We thought you'd like new outfits for the concert, so we're taking you to Harwoods," he smiled.

"Wow!" gasped Rachel. "The most famous department store in the city!"

While the adults chatted, Kirsty whispered in Rachel's ear. "What about the Keepsake Key? I really want to visit Harwoods, but we must help

Destiny get her other two magical objects back. Jack Frost and his goblins can't be allowed to ruin pop music forever!" But before there was time to think, the girls were whisked off on their shopping trip.

Inside the magnificent store, Rachel and Kirsty travelled up the long escalators, feeling very excited. The fashion department was huge. As their parents wandered around, the girls hurried eagerly towards a rack of colourful sparkly clothes.

"Perfect!" said Rachel, holding up a pretty skirt and distracting Kirsty. "This would look great on you!"

"And this would be just right for you," replied Kirsty, pulling out a pair of jeans with a sequin trim.

Suddenly a group of children in hooded tops pushed past them. "Hey," cried Kirsty. "Be careful!"

"It's odd to see children on their own," said Rachel thoughtfully, walking into the changing rooms.

The girls tried on their outfits, and as they were putting on their own clothes again, Kirsty froze.

Poking out from the bottom of the next cubicle was a pair of green feet!

"I'm sure that's a goblin!" Rachel hissed,

pulling open the curtain. At
first the goblin inside didn't
notice. He was wearing a
purple suit and a striped
waistcoat. As the girls
watched, he raised his
hat and admired himself
in the mirror. Kirsty
and Rachel burst out
laughing and watched the
goblin's green cheeks turn red.

"You horrible girls!" he
stammered. "How dare you laugh at
me!" He stuck his tongue out at them and
shot off in a rage. The girls hurried after him,
but ran straight into their parents, who were
waiting outside.

"Now, let's look at the shoes," said Mrs
Tate, smiling.

Rachel and Kirsty would have to give up the
chase for now.

As they headed up to the next floor on the
escalator, the girls spotted three small figures
wearing wigs running up and down, laughing
and getting in everyone's way.

"What's going on?" a security guard
suddenly demanded.

"Run!" shrieked a figure in a blonde wig, as he led the others towards the music department.

The girls chose their shoes quickly, then asked if they could look round on their own.

"All right," said Mrs Walker. "We'll meet you in the café."

As the girls headed off, Rachel noticed a mirror tucked away in a quiet corner, fizzing and sparkling. As she peered into it, a small figure burst through. It was Destiny! She smiled as she waved her wand and shrank the girls to fairy size.

"Follow me!" she said urgently, flying quickly towards the electrical department.

With a wave of her wand, The Angels appeared
on every TV screen, sitting in their dressing
room looking glum.

The girls looked confused as Destiny
explained. "The Keepsake Key protects pop stars'
songs. Every copy of the music for The Angels'
new song has been stolen, and they've got to sing
it tonight!"

"We're not going to let Jack Frost spoil everything," said Kirsty in a determined tone. "Come on, let's find those goblins and make them give back the Keepsake Key!"

When they reached the music department, everything seemed calm and quiet. "Maybe they've gone," Rachel suggested.

"No – listen!" said Kirsty.

The girls could hear a squeaking sound which grew louder and louder, until around the corner sped a unicycle with a squeaky wheel, ridden by a goblin in a long silky dress. Behind him was another on a pogo stick wearing pyjamas, and a third wobbling along on roller blades.

"Look at what that goblin on the pogo stick has around his neck," Destiny said, excitedly.

"It's my Keepsake Key!"

"I think I can unfasten it and fly away," Rachel whispered, ducking behind the goblin's shoulders and fluttering her wings as she tried to undo the chain.

"Something's tickling my neck!" whined the goblin, whirling around and spotting Rachel. "Look! A fairy is trying to steal the key!" He yanked the chain from around his neck and tucked it into his pyjama pocket.

"Run!" bellowed the goblin on roller blades, as they zoomed into the toy department.

There were children everywhere, but suddenly the girls heard a shriek.

"Look!" Rachel exclaimed as they saw the three goblins staring in fear at a guide dog.

"Silly goblins!" said Rachel. "Guide dogs are the gentlest dogs in the world!"

Destiny giggled, but Kirsty was looking thoughtful. "Did you see those battery-powered dogs?" she whispered, smiling. "Perhaps we can distract the goblins with them!"

"That's a great idea!" said Destiny with a smile.

She used magic to create a cloud of colourful balloons to distract the children, while the girls flitted around, shepherding the goblins closer and closer to the yapping toy dogs.

"Eeek!" the goblins squealed. "Look at the hairy monsters! Help!"

"Goblins!" said Destiny, fluttering above them. "Please return the Keepsake Key."

"No!" squeaked the smallest goblin.

At that moment one of the toy dogs yapped loudly, flipped over and landed in the lap of the goblin with the Keepsake Key.

He screamed in terror, pulled the key from his pocket and threw it to Destiny, who shrank it to fairy size, catching it neatly.

"Thank you," she said, rising high into the air. "And by the way, those 'monsters' are just toys!"

"What?" roared the smallest goblin. "You tricksy fairies!"

Destiny and the girls fluttered back into the electrical department. "Thank you," the little fairy said. "I have to take the key to Fairyland but I'll be back soon. We still have to find the Magical Microphone!"

Destiny returned the girls to human size, then disappeared in a shower of glitter.

A second later, The Angels appeared on the TV screens again, smiling this time. "Our song!" laughed Emilia, waving their sheet music around.

"Our music's been found!"

Soon, the Christmas lights were due to be switched on. Then it would be time for the concert. Just one more magical object to find!

The Magical Microphone

Rachel and Kirsty quickly changed, ready for the switching on of the Christmas lights and the concert.

"Come on, girls!" called Mrs Tate, and a few seconds later, the two families hurried down to the hotel lobby.

Their parents left the hotel to make their own way, while the girls rushed over to The Angels, who were waiting for them in the lobby.

"Girls, you look great!" said Serena, giving them each a hug. "Come on, our car's here!"

They led the girls out of the hotel. A long,

pink Cadillac was waiting for them, with a smart chauffeur at the wheel. Jumping in with The Angels, Rachel and Kirsty felt like pop stars themselves! "We're so excited about turning on the lights," Emilia told them. "It's such a special occasion."

As they set off, Serena pointed at a scooter riding alongside them in the traffic. Kirsty and Rachel looked out of the window and saw six goblins standing on the back of it in a pyramid shape.

"Oh no!" groaned Kirsty in a low, worried voice. "Rachel, look at the driver!"

It was Jack Frost!

"Oh no!" whispered

Rachel in Kirsty's ear.

He's got the Magical Microphone!" As they watched, Jack Frost roared away on his bike.

The goblins held on until suddenly, the goblin at the top began to wobble and lost his balance. He fell off the scooter, and into the middle of the road!

"Luckily everyone's wearing fancy dress for the ceremony," whispered Kirsty. "People will think he's in a costume." The girls watched as the goblin leapt to his feet, and disappeared into the crowd.

Suddenly their car began to rattle, and then stopped.

"That's not good," said Lexy as the chauffeur and The Angels got out to see what was wrong.

"Kirsty, look!" Rachel cried in excitement. The gear stick was glowing and there, on the top of it, was Destiny!

"Destiny, Jack Frost is here in the human world and we can't follow him!" Kirsty blurted out, almost before Destiny could speak.

She waved her
wand and the car
started up.

"The car broke
down because the
Magical Microphone
is missing," Destiny
explained. "It keeps
all technical things
around pop stars
running smoothly."

Looking relieved, The Angels and the
chauffeur jumped back into the car as Destiny
dived into Rachel's handbag. They arrived at the
podium with seconds to spare.

Rachel and Kirsty scanned the crowd,
searching for Jack Frost.

"We are thrilled," Serena said to the crowd, "to be turning on the Christmas lights this year."

As the girls were about to press the button, Kirsty gripped Rachel's hand. "I see him!" she exclaimed excitedly.

Jack was standing at the edge of the crowd.

Before the girls could think what to do, he stuck out his tongue, then tapped his wand against the Magical Microphone. All the lights went out, leaving Main Street in darkness. The crowd gasped.

Destiny quickly flew out of Rachel's bag. The girls didn't see her wave her wand, but they both felt themselves shrinking to fairy size. They all held hands together and rose into the air. The lights in the side streets were still on,

and almost at once Rachel spotted a green leg disappearing through the side door of the theatre.

"This way!" she cried. Inside, the lights were down and a musical was in full swing. They split up and began to search around the theatre. Luckily it was dark and everyone was looking at the stage. Suddenly. Kirsty grabbed the others' hands and pointed. Jack Frost was sitting in the back row with five of his goblins.

They were making so much noise that they were disturbing everyone around them.

"They haven't seen us," said Kirsty. "Let's creep up and try to find the Magical Microphone."

"Boo!" shouted Jack Frost rudely.

"Rubbish!" shouted a goblin.

"They're spoiling the show for everyone!" cried Destiny.

Someone had obviously complained because just then some stewards arrived and pinned Jack Frost's arms to his side.

"Lemme go!" wailed a goblin as another steward seized him by the shoulders.

"I don't care how much effort you've put into these silly costumes," hissed the chief steward. "We're not putting up with this any longer."

Jack Frost and the goblins were hauled off and thrown out of the building. Rachel quickly flew over to where they had been, and found the Magical Microphone under Jack Frost's seat! Destiny waved her wand and returned it to Fairyland size.

A minute later, the three friends landed back on the podium in Main Street, next to The Angels. "Thank you so much!" said Destiny happily.

"Now I must rush to Fairyland with the Magical Microphone!" And with a sprinkle of fairy dust, she returned the girls to their normal size.

"Happy Christmas, everyone!" shouted The Angels, Rachel and Kirsty as they pressed the big red button together. The lights flashed on, and the crowd cheered.

The concert that evening was spectacular, and at the end, Rachel and Kirsty went backstage to say goodbye to The Angels and thank them.

"I'm so sleepy!" yawned Rachel as they changed into their pyjamas in the hotel room. "Oh, Kirsty – look!"

On each of their pillows was a silver mirror, and on the back of each was an inscription that said, "With love and thanks, Destiny xx".

When they looked into the glass of the mirror,

they could see her waving at them, with King Oberon and Queen Titania behind her.

"Thank you, and goodnight, everyone!" Rachel whispered. "See you again soon!"

The girls snuggled down into their beds.

"We've had lots of exciting adventures," murmured Kirsty. "But this has been the most star-studded one yet!"

Flora the Fancy Dress Fairy

The
Fairyland
Palace

The Great Cake

"What a beautiful place!" Rachel Walker cried when she saw McKersey Castle. Her grown-up cousin Lindsay was having a party there to celebrate her wedding anniversary and Rachel was invited, along with her best friend, Kirsty Tate.

"It's just like a fairytale castle," Rachel said.

Kirsty grinned. They knew all about fairies because they had helped them many times!

Inside the castle, Lindsay showed the girls to their bedroom.

Rachel and Kirsty gasped with delight when they saw the huge room.

Lindsay pointed to a small door set opposite the beds. "That door leads up to the battlements," she said. "Be careful if you go up there!"

As Lindsay hurried off, Rachel opened the little

door and found a staircase winding upwards.

Suddenly a chilly gust of wind blew right down into the room.

"Look, there's ice all over the stairs!" Kirsty gasped in amazement.

The girls were curious, so they climbed the steps, holding on to the handrail. The higher they got, the colder they felt.

"My Icicle Party will be the best fun ever!" snapped an icy voice ahead of them.

The two girls crept to the top of the steps.

They saw Jack Frost standing there!

"I'll be the one having a party tomorrow, not those pesky humans!"

he said to the goblin servant beside him.

"We can't let Jack Frost spoil our party," said Kirsty. "Let's go to Fairyland and get help!"

The girls opened their special lockets and sprinkled fairy dust over their heads. The magical dust turned them into fairies and whisked them away.

As soon as Rachel and Kirsty landed in
Fairyland, a fairy in a fabulous mermaid
costume flew up to them.

"Oh, I'm so glad to see you!" she cried. "I'm
Flora the Fancy
Dress Fairy."

The girls
said, "Hello!"

"Is
something
wrong?" Kirsty
asked.

"Some goblins
have stolen my magical
items," Flora said. "I need them to make
sure fancy dress parties go well. The magical
figurine, a little golden model of a princess,

makes food taste wonderful. The Red Riding
Hood cape helps costumes look good and the
third item is a mask with rainbow feathers that
makes sure everyone has a fun time."

Rachel and Kirsty looked at each other
in alarm.

"Flora, we know where your items might be!"
said Kirsty. "I bet Jack Frost's goblins have taken
them for his Icicle Party!"

"Then I'll magic you back to McKersey Castle, and we can all search for them," said Flora.

The girls were swept up in a cloud of fairy dust. A moment later, they found themselves standing on top of the castle.

Kirsty looked over the stone battlements at a van that was parked below.

"Look, goblins!" she said.

The cake shop van had its back doors open. As the girls and Flora watched, they saw three goblins climbing out. The goblins had a big cardboard box and they tore it open.

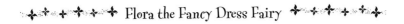

Inside was a big white cake. On top there was a little figurine.

"They're stealing Lindsay's cake!" Rachel wailed.

"And my magic figurine!" said Flora. "Without it, all the food at the party will be spoiled!"

Flora whizzed down to talk to the cheeky goblins.

"Go away, pesky fairies!" said one of the goblins. "We're taking this cake for Jack Frost's Icicle Party."

He broke off chunks of cake and threw them at Flora and the girls.

"He's ruining it!" Kirsty gasped.

Then the other two goblins began eating the cake with their hands.

"Yum!" they said.

"Stop that!" the first goblin shouted. "Jack Frost's waiting for us."

"We should put the cake in the van," said another goblin.

The girls and Flora saw a different van parked nearby. It had 'Jack Frost's Frosted Delights' written on the side. The goblins ran over to it and began struggling to put what was left of the cake inside.

Flora, Rachel and Kirsty wondered how they could stop the goblins getting away.

Suddenly Rachel had an idea. "If we lift up the drawbridge, they won't be able to leave the castle!"

"Brilliant!" said Kirsty.

The goblins had climbed into their van and were driving it away. But Flora waved her wand and pointed it at the drawbridge.

Magical sparks flew around the chains and the drawbridge lifted up.

The goblins were trapped inside the castle!

"Thanks, Flora!" said Rachel. "Let's get the cake!"

Quickly, Flora turned Rachel and Kirsty back to human size. But before they could get to the van, the goblins opened the back door.

"All right, have your stupid cake!" one sneered.
They pushed the cake out – SPLAT!

"Oh no!" cried Rachel.

The cake was ruined. But Flora's figurine was still in one piece.

"Those silly goblins forgot about the Icicle Party and just wanted to upset us," said Kirsty.

"Don't worry," whispered Flora. "Just wait until I get my magic figurine back."

Flora lowered the drawbridge. The goblins zoomed out of the castle in their van, blowing raspberries at the girls.

As soon as the van was gone, Flora flew over to her figurine.

"Now, close your eyes and make a wish," she said.

The girls held hands and wished for the most beautiful cake ever made. When they opened their eyes again, it was standing in front of them!

Colourful Costumes

The day of the anniversary party had arrived.

"I'll show you the costumes," Lindsay said to Rachel and Kirsty. "You can have first pick!"

Kirsty and Rachel followed Lindsay down a staircase and along a corridor to a sturdy wooden door.

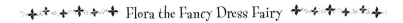

"Enjoy choosing your outfits," she said. "I have to go and prepare for the party!"

"This will be fun," said Kirsty. She pushed open the door.

But the girls were shocked when they saw what was inside!

Two goblins were pulling costumes off racks and throwing them around the room.

"Stop that!" cried Rachel.

The room was a total mess. One rack had been knocked over, and the costumes were lying in a heap. The goblins saw the girls and grabbed piles of clothes. Then they climbed onto the window ledge.

"They're going to jump!" Kirsty shouted.

The goblins leapt out of the window and held onto a heavy rope which had been tied to a wardrobe.

The girls rushed to see where they had gone.

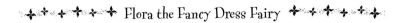

"Look!" Kirsty cried. She pointed at a boat in the moat.

In it were three goblins, ready to row it away. "They've got Flora's magic cape!" Rachel gasped. She had spotted a piece of bright red material in the boat.

"Let's get onto the drawbridge and grab the cape as the goblins row past," Kirsty said.

The girls dashed down the stairs, and passed a suit of armour with an open visor. They could see a strange, sparkly glow inside. It was Flora!

"Hello, girls!" said the fairy as she flew out of the helmet. "Where are you going?"

Rachel quickly told Flora what had happened and the three friends hurried to the drawbridge.

"We're going to lean over and grab the cape," Kirsty said.

"Good plan!" Flora replied.

Rachel and Kirsty lay down on the drawbridge. The boat with the goblins was close. Rachel reached out to snatch the sparkling red cape, but one of the goblins spotted them!

"They're trying to steal our costumes!" a big goblin yelled. "Stop rowing around in a circle! Let's go to the bank!"

Kirsty, Rachel and Flora watched in dismay as the goblins rowed away.

"I nearly got the cape, too," Rachel said.

The girls ran across the drawbridge. They were hoping to catch the goblins on the other side.

The goblins reached the bank and threw the costumes out of the boat.

"There are too many to carry!" one of the goblins shouted.

"Put on some of the clothes!" another goblin said.

Flora and the girls watched in surprise as the goblins dressed themselves up. They looked ridiculous!

The costumes were far too big for the goblins. They had been designed for humans! One goblin put on a tiger outfit and a clown's nose.

Another was wearing a pink wig with a golden crown on top. He also had Flora's magic cape tied around his neck. But the hood kept falling forwards over his face! All of them were wearing odd shoes and kept tripping up.

Flora, Rachel and Kirsty couldn't help laughing as they crossed the drawbridge. "Give us those costumes!" Flora called.

"No!" came the reply. "Jack Frost's holding *his* party here tonight, so you won't need them for *your* party!"

Another goblin cackled in glee, then threw a dress over Rachel, Kirsty and Flora.

"Help!" Rachel cried, trying to struggle free.

The girls quickly untangled themselves from the dress. But by then the goblins had already run off.

They had left lots of costumes behind them on the ground.

"We can't leave them but there are too many to carry," said Rachel. She pointed at the scattered clothes.

Kirsty looked closely at a pretty jacket.

"The stitching on this is coming loose!" she cried.

"The costumes are falling apart because my magic cape is missing," Flora explained. "If we get it back, I can fix them!"

"Can you shrink the clothes to pocket size?" Kirsty asked.

With a wave of her wand, Flora made the clothes tiny. The girls put them in their pockets.

Then they all rushed after the goblins. They
ran towards a steep slope where some goats
were grazing.

"Perhaps we can ask the goats to help us,"
Rachel suggested.

"Great idea!" Flora said. "Animals like fairies."

Flora whispered to the goats. They looked up
and then trotted over to the goblins. They were
blocking their path!

The goblins stared nervously at the hairy creatures. They shook with fear.

"They're very big," said one goblin.

"Do you think they eat goblins?" asked another.

One of the goblins was wearing a hat with a felt flower. A curious goat came over to sniff it.

"Baaa!" said the goat, and tried to eat the flower.

The goblins were terrified! They threw down all the costumes they were carrying and backed away in fear.

"What the goats really want is the clothes!"
Flora told the girls. "They like to eat cloth."

The goats started sniffing the goblins all over.
The goblins pulled off their clothes and held
them out. They wailed in fear.

"Don't eat me!" begged the goblin with the
cape. "This cloak is much tastier than I am."

The goat snorted. Yelling with fear, the goblin threw down the cape and ran away. His terrified friends followed.

Quickly, Flora shrank the clothes and the girls gathered them up. Then they ran back to the castle. Flora began to sort out the mess in the room where the costumes were kept.

As the little fairy flicked her magic wand,

Rachel and Kirsty watched the clothes grow back to normal size and tidy themselves up.

"I must take my magic cape back to Fairyland," said Flora with a smile. "Meanwhile, you two need to get dressed for the party. Somewhere in this room my magic has sorted out perfect costumes for you!"

Rachel and Kirsty grinned at each other.

"Let's see what we can find!" Kirsty said.

The Perfect Party

"Look, Rachel!" cried Kirsty. She had spotted tiny magical sparkles shimmering around a clothes rail.

Hanging on the rail were two angel costumes. They were absolutely perfect!

The girls got dressed and went down to the ballroom. The decorations were white and gold.

Marble statues wearing masks had been placed around the walls. The cake stood on a table in the middle.

"It's beautiful!" Kirsty said.

"I don't think any of these masks are Flora's magic one," said Rachel. "We must find it before the goblins do. Otherwise the party will be totally ruined!"

"Look up there," Kirsty cried. She pointed at the figurine on the top of the cake. "It's Flora!"

The figurine winked. But they didn't have time to say hello. Some rather odd guests had arrived.

"Goblins!" Rachel gasped.

"We're here for Jack Frost's party!" snapped one of the smartly dressed guests.

He was holding up an invitation. "It's taking place here, tonight."

The girls glanced nervously at the invitation. It clearly read 'McKersey Castle'.

"Tell him to check it again!" Flora whispered.

She waved her wand at the invitation.

The goblin re-read the fancy invitation and his eyes almost popped out of his head.

"It says the party is at Jack Frost's Ice Castle!" he muttered.

The goblins all turned and left, miserably. It was just in time. Lindsay's real guests were arriving for her party.

"Grrr!" A growl made the girls look round.

They saw a woman dressed as a tiger spring forward. She began sharpening her claws on a pillar.

"She's taking the dressing-up a bit too seriously!" Rachel whispered to Kirsty.

"People's costumes are going wrong because my mask is missing," said Flora sadly. "Your fairy lockets are protecting you, but not the other guests. That woman thinks she actually is a tiger!"

Suddenly Lindsay rushed in. She looked upset. She was still wearing ordinary clothes.

"I went to put my costume on but I can't find my mask!" Lindsay said.

"We have to find the magic mask quickly," whispered Rachel. "Let's go and search!"

The girls tiptoed away from the party and began looking around the castle.

The girls walked up and down all the corridors of the castle, but they found nothing.

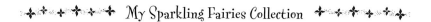

Then Kirsty spotted something pink at the bottom of a staircase.

"Look, goblin footprints – and a tiny little feather!" she said.

"It's from my magic mask!" whispered Flora.

The footprints seemed to stop dead right in front of a wall.

"Do you think there's a secret passage?" Rachel asked.

The girls peered at the wall until Kirsty spotted a hole.

Kirsty put her hand into the hole and felt a little switch. When she pressed it, the wall swung back.

The three friends stared into a dark passageway.

Rachel and Flora followed Kirsty down the narrow corridor. But they just found a dead end.

"This is no good," said Kirsty.

"Let me check this wall," Rachel replied. She felt the stones and found another hole with a switch inside it.

Rachel pressed the switch and the wall moved a few centimetres, as if it was a door.

The girls peered into a cave-like room. They could see a familiar figure sitting on a throne. He had the magic mask in his hand.

"Jack Frost!" Kirsty said.

"We're going to ruin this pesky party!" Jack Frost said. He laughed nastily.

Kirsty opened the door a bit wider, and saw lots of goblins listening to Jack Frost.

"I'll run in and grab the mask," Kirsty said, trying to feel brave. She crept into the room. Jack Frost was shouting and waving the mask about.

Kirsty was able to snatch it easily!

"Stop that girl!" Jack Frost roared. But Rachel had already pulled the door closed behind Kirsty. He was too late!

The girls and Flora ran down the passage. A few moments later they were back at the party.

"I can see Lindsay and Robert," Kirsty said. She pointed to a couple who were wearing fantastic king and queen costumes.

"Lindsay!" Kirsty called. "We found your mask."

"How dare you talk to me in such a rude manner?" Lindsay snapped.

Rachel and Kirsty stared at each other in confusion. "It's OK," Flora whispered. "She thinks she's a real queen. Try giving her my magic mask. It will help."

"Your Majesty," said Rachel. "We have brought you this tribute!" She held out the mask.

Lindsay took it, and held it up to her face. She blinked, then seemed to wake up, as though she'd been in a dream.

The girls were delighted. Lindsay was back to normal, and soon the party was in full swing.

All three of Flora's magic items had been found, so everything was sure to go well.

"Look over there!" said Kirsty. She pointed to someone dressed as a pirate. He had a spiky beard. With him were other guests with green faces.

"What amazing face paint!" the woman in the tiger costume said to them.

"Even Jack Frost and his goblins are joining in the fancy dress party!" Kirsty laughed.

"Thank you so much for all your help, girls," Flora said. "I'm going to stay for the party to make sure it goes perfectly."

And it did!

Florence the Friendship Fairy

The Fairyland Palace

Maypole

Band stand

Stalls

Treasure hunt

Kirsty's House

Wetherbury Village

Magical Memories

Rachel Walker was staying with her best friend
Kirsty Tate. One day they looked through Kirsty's
scrapbook, which was full of lovely things.

Kirsty and Rachel had a special secret. They
were friends with the fairies! The scrapbook
reminded them of all the fun they'd had together.

"I hope we'll have another fairy adventure soon," Kirsty whispered.

Then she frowned.

"There's an empty space here. I don't remember that," she said.

Worse still, when Rachel turned the next page she saw that one photo was damaged. Another one looked unfamiliar.

"I don't recognise her," said Rachel. She pointed to a picture of a fairy.

Before either girl could say another word, the fairy began to sparkle. She flew straight out from the page!

"Hello, Rachel and Kirsty!" the little fairy beamed. I'm Florence the Friendship Fairy. My magical memory book protects people's special memories."

"How lovely," said Kirsty. "But I don't think the magic is working at the moment."

Rachel held up the damaged scrapbook, and Florence looked at it sadly.

"My memory book has been stolen by naughty goblins," she said. "So your scrapbook is no longer magically protected!"

"That's terrible!" said Kirsty.

"Goblins have come here and messed up your book," Florence said. "I must find them before they do more damage."

"We'll help!" Rachel promised.

Just then, Kirsty's mum came into the room and asked the girls to go to the village shop to buy some groceries. Florence had to hide in the scrapbook!

A few minutes later the girls headed into the village with Florence. Rachel soon spotted something on the ground.

"That's a picture from my scrapbook!" said Kirsty.

The girls were walking together through the park when they heard the sound of people squabbling.

They hid behind a bush and saw three goblins
marching along, pushing each other as they went.
One of them was carrying a smart-looking book.

"That's my magical memory book!"
whispered Florence.

"Why don't we make a memory book?" said a
small goblin. "It would be far better than this one.
I've got lots of lovely dirt and weeds to put in it!"

"We should put in a photo of me ripping up this soppy fairy book!" another goblin sniggered.

"No!" cried Florence, flying out from behind the bush. "Don't do that!"

"Go away," one of the goblins snapped. "We're not letting a silly fairy interfere."

The goblins sprinted away, one of them still holding the magical memory book. As he ran, all Florence's treasures began to fall from the pages.

"They're ruining it!" she cried.

She swooped down and waved her wand,

making all the items fairy-size and collecting everything that had fallen out.

The girls quickly followed the goblins.

The goblins kept banging into each other, but didn't stop.

"How do we make them drop the book?" asked Florence.

"I know," said Rachel.

Then she shouted at the goblins: "Look out! There are hundreds of fairies following right behind you!"

"They're going to cover you in beautiful pink sparkles and take a photo!" added Kirsty.

"Yuck! Run for it!" cried the goblins. They were too silly to turn around and see that there was only one fairy fluttering along beside Kirsty and Rachel.

But the goblin carrying the magical memory book didn't drop it, as the girls had hoped. Instead, he clutched it even more tightly.

The goblins ducked down a side street with Florence and the girls following closely behind them.

Kirsty grinned when she saw the road was a dead end!

Moments later, the goblins all had their backs to the wall.

The smallest one was still clutching the magical memory book.

"Why do you want my pink book, anyway?" Florence asked them. "Wouldn't you rather have a nice green one instead?"

"Of course we would," said another goblin. "But we haven't got a green book, so we're having yours!"

The goblin stuck out his tongue at the girls and Florence.

"If we could find you the perfect goblin memory book, with an icky green cover, would you do a swap?" Rachel asked.

The goblins looked thoughtful.

"I could make you one with prickly bits and slime patches," Florence said. "I could even use magic so you could add your favourite smells.

But only if you give me my book back."

"Oh, could you make it smell like dirty feet?" one asked.

"Mouldy mushrooms, too!" said another.

"I want blocked drains!" cried the third.

Florence nodded.

"It's a deal," they said.

Florence waved her wand and an oozy green book appeared.

She gave it to them in return for her book.

"Thanks, girls!" she said to Kirsty and Rachel. "I have to go now, but take a look in your bag."

As Florence vanished, Kirsty reached inside her mum's bag. She pulled out two invitations.

"Rachel!" she cried. "We're invited to a Friendship Party at the Fairyland Palace!"

The Friendship
Party

The next day was the grand opening of a new
Friendship Hall in Wetherbury, the village where
Kirsty lived. The girls were helping Mrs Tate hang
decorations for it.

Suddenly, Florence flew in through an open
window. She looked pale and anxious.

"Some goblins have stolen my magical friendship ribbon!" she said. "Without it, our Fairy Friendship Party will be a flop. Will you help me? We need to search Fairyland for the goblins."

"We'd love to," said Kirsty. "But we're helping my mum."

"I can cast a spell so that time stands still while you're away," said Florence.

"Brilliant!" Rachel replied.

With a shimmer of sparkles Florence transformed the girls into fairies, and whisked them away to Fairyland.

When Rachel and Kirsty reached Fairyland, they were pleased to see some old friends.

"It's Phoebe the Fashion Fairy!" said Kirsty.

The girls waved to Phoebe.

Their fairy friend was pushing a rail of party dresses. When she waved back to the girls, several dresses slipped off their hangers.

Then Zoe the Skating Fairy whizzed up and rollerskated right over the dresses! She dropped the box of china plates she was carrying.

CRASH!

"All the party preparations are going wrong because I've lost my magic ribbon!" wailed the little fairy.

"Where is it usually kept?" Kirsty asked.

"It's normally tied to the maypole," Florence explained.

The girls saw a golden pole and walked over to look at it.

"The goblins decided they wanted to play with the ribbon, and stole it," said Florence.

"We'll help find it," Rachel promised.

"Those naughty goblins can't be far away!"

The three fairies fluttered into the air and began searching. A horrible burning smell floated up to them from the Fairyland bakery.

Things were going wrong wherever they looked.

As the fairies were flying over some woods, they heard loud shouts and cheers. They swooped down and ducked behind a tree trunk.

There were the goblins!

They were using Florence's beautiful friendship ribbon for a tug-of-war game.

"Oh no, they'll rip it!" cried poor Florence.

Then the goblins dropped the ribbon and started squabbling over who had won the game.

"Never mind that," said the biggest goblin. "How about a game of blind man's buff? We can use the ribbon as a blindfold."

As the goblins began to play, one of them picked up a pile of acorns and threw them hard at his blindfolded friend.

"Ow!" wailed the goblin who had been hurt.

"Ha ha!" jeered another.

"I really need to get that ribbon," whispered Florence to the girls. "But how?"

Kirsty had an idea.

"I know just what to do!" she said.

"Florence, could you magic up two ordinary ribbons that look like your friendship ribbon?" Kirsty went on.

"Of course," said the fairy.

"We're going to suggest to the goblins that they have a three-legged race," Kirsty said. "They can use the ribbons to tie up their legs. Then we trip them up and grab the magical friendship ribbon back!"

Florence waved her wand until two matching ribbons appeared in a swirl of sparkles.

"Yoo hoo!" Rachel called to the goblins.
"Why don't you have a three-legged race?"

The goblins thought a race would be exciting.

"We'll show you soppy fairies how to have fun!" one sneered.

The goblins tied their legs together and ran off. But Florence made acorns appear magically under their feet.

The goblins wailed as they tripped and fell over.

"Quick!" Rachel cried. "Grab the ribbon!"

Florence zoomed through the air and quickly untied her magical friendship ribbon from the tangle of goblin legs.

"Got it!" she said. "Come on, let's fly back and tie it to the maypole!"

The goblins yelled and shook their fists at the fairies, but Florence, Kirsty and Rachel soared out of their reach.

The three of them flew all the way back to the maypole, where Florence proudly tied the ribbon back in its place.

"Hurrah!" cheered everyone.

"Is that Kirsty and Rachel I see?" came a booming voice from behind them.

The girls turned around to see King Oberon and Queen Titania coming across the grass towards the maypole.

Kirsty and Rachel smiled back politely at the royal fairies, and bobbed curtseys.

Florence explained how Kirsty and Rachel

had helped her rescue the magical memory book and the magical friendship ribbon.

"All the fairies are grateful for your help," said Queen Titania, "We would be very honoured if you two could officially open our party."

Kirsty and Rachel joined hands and grinned.

"We declare the Fairy Friendship Party OPEN!" they said together.

Rachel and Kirsty had a wonderful time at the party until it was time to go home.

"Goodbye for now, girls," said Florence. "Later on, I'll bring you a thank-you present!"

She waved her wand and a whirlwind of magical sparkles rose up. When they disappeared, the girls saw they were back in Wetherbury Friendship Hall, holding the banner they had been going to hang on the wall.

"Look!" Rachel said, pointing at the painted letters on the banner. Before they had been plain, but now they were decorated with sparkly glitter.

"Fairy magic," Kirsty whispered, and the girls shared a smile.

Friends Forever

"I'm really looking forward to this!" said Rachel. She and Kirsty were preparing for a party to celebrate the opening of Wetherbury's new hall.

To make things even more exciting, Florence the Friendship Fairy had promised to bring the girls a present to thank them for rescuing two of her magical obects from naughty goblins.

The girls walked in to find that the party had already begun. But something seemed to be wrong.

"Nobody seems to be enjoying themselves," said Kirsty. She looked around.

There were sour expressions on all the children's faces.

Suddenly the girls saw Florence flutter out from behind a plant.

"It's my fault everyone's miserable," said the fairy. "I made a special friendship bracelet for each of you, and I was going to give them to you today."

"How lovely!" said Rachel. "But how does that make it your fault that the party is going badly?"

"A goblin stole the bracelets," explained Florence, sadly.

"A friendship bracelet should only be worn by the person it was made for," the fairy explained. "Otherwise the magic goes wrong, and people nearby start arguing."

"Do you think the goblin who stole our bracelets is here at the party?" cried Rachel.

"He must be," said Florence.

The friends looked around the hall.

A magician was just getting ready to perform his tricks, and the grumpy children were sitting down to watch.

"There's the goblin!" Kirsty said, pointing.

A goblin with a pointy nose was sitting in the front row, dressed as a wizard. He was wearing a colourful bracelet!

The magician put on a good show, but nobody looked impressed. Before long he hurried off stage. The sulky children wandered away, too. Only the goblin stayed behind.

"I want to see some proper magic!" he grumbled, looking cross.

"We could use proper magic to trick him," suggested Kirsty. "Florence, can you magic us up magicians' costumes, please?"

The goblin looked surprised when the girls walked over to him in magical-looking colourful robes.

"Abracadabra!" said Kirsty, and a dove flew out of her hat!

"Wow!" said the goblin.

He didn't know Florence was hidden under Rachel's hair, doing all the magic for Kirsty.

"If you want to see a really good trick, watch my wand carefully," Kirsty said.

The goblin stared eagerly at the wand. Suddenly, a string of silk handkerchiefs shot out of its tip and swirled around his arms!

The handkerchiefs tightened around him.

"What's happening?" he cried, trying to raise his trapped arms.

"We're taking Florence's bracelet back!" replied Kirsty. She untied it from his wrist.

Two other goblins hurried into the room. When they saw the tied-up goblin, they released him at once.

"You'll never find the other one!" a goblin sneered. "I hid it in this chest I found, in . . ."

"Ssh, don't tell them!" snapped the first goblin.

"What chest?" said Florence. "Where is it?"

The goblins said nothing.

Kirsty, Rachel and Florence went outside to search for the chest.

Kirsty's mum was outside, talking to the other children. They all looked happier now that the magic of the first friendship bracelet was working.

"We're having a treasure hunt," said Mrs Tate. "Follow the clues to find the chest!"

"We have to find that chest first!" said Rachel to Kirsty. "Florence, can you turn us into fairies so we can fly?"

"The first clue is 'chair'," said Mrs Tate, as Florence waved her wand and the girls shrank.

The treasure hunt clues were hidden all around the garden and the hall. Each time you found one, it told you where to look for the next.

The girls took great care not to be spotted by any of the other children. They fluttered under all the chairs in the hall, looking for one with a clue stuck to it. When they found the clue, it said to look for a balloon next, and when they found the clue on the balloon, that one told them to look among the trees.

"Look!" cried Kirsty, as the three fairies flew past a big tree. Nestled among the tree's roots was a small, sturdy chest. Its lid was open – and there, on top of a big pile of chocolate coins, was the missing friendship bracelet!

Florence turned both girls back to normal,
and they proudly slipped the friendship bracelets
onto their wrists.

"Thank you so much, Florence," said Rachel.

Then they went to share the chocolate coins with all the children at the party!

After everyone had eaten their fill, a band started playing so people could dance.

Florence hid behind Rachel's hair, and watched the fun.

"I have to go back to Fairyland now,"

she said. "But I'm so glad I met you both."

"Thanks, Florence," Kirsty said. "I really love my bracelet!"

"Me too," Rachel said.

Florence blew them a kiss and vanished in a puff of sparkles.

"Hooray for friends," Kirsty said, holding Rachel's hand.

"And hooray for fairies," replied Rachel. "I wonder what adventures we'll have next?"

Belle the
Birthday
Fairy

Jack Frost's
Ice Castle

Road to Ice
Castle ↓

Village
Hall ↓

Rachel's
House

Skate Park

The Birthday Book

"I can't wait to see Mum's face when she arrives at her surprise party!" Rachel Walker said as she and her best friend, Kirsty Tate, happily swung their roller skates on their way to the park.

"She'll be amazed when she realises that you and your dad arranged it all!" Kirsty grinned.

She was staying at Rachel's house in Tippington for half-term, and for the party.

"Everything's ready," Rachel went on, "the food, the music, the decorations for the village hall. And Dad's ordered a cake from the baker's."

As they passed the village hall, where the party was to be held, Rachel squeezed Kirsty's hand. "Let's have a quick look inside," she said.

"Ooh, yes!" replied Kirsty eagerly, and they put their heads around the door.

A group of party guests were there, but no one was having much fun. The parents were clearing up squashed cakes and spilled drinks, and instead of playing music, the CD player was making strange whining sounds. Rachel and Kirsty looked around, and saw a little girl in a pink dress looking sad.

"Is this your party?" Rachel asked her.

"Yes." She nodded sadly. "But everything's gone wrong. We can't even dance!"

The two older girls were both doing their best to comfort her.

When they got to the park, the girls put on their skates. But they both still felt upset about the little girl's party being ruined.

"If only one of the Party Fairies had been here, they could have helped," Kirsty sighed.

The girls were good friends with the fairies, often helping them outwit bad-tempered Jack Frost and his naughty goblin servants.

"You're right!" said a musical voice close by. Peering into a hedge, the girls saw a tiny fairy sitting cross-legged. She had long brown hair and was wearing a pretty purple dress, with sparkly gold ballet pumps.

"Hi, girls!" She smiled. "I'm Belle the Birthday Fairy, and I need your help!"

"Hi, Belle!" said Rachel and Kirsty together. "What's wrong?"

"Jack Frost has stolen my birthday charms, and we must get them back!"

Belle explained that the birthday charms make sure birthdays go smoothly in Fairyland and the human world. With the charms in Jack Frost's hands, birthdays everywhere were going wrong.

"Will you come to Fairyland and help look?"

asked Belle.

"Of course!" Kirsty and Rachel cried together.

Belle waved her wand and multicoloured sparkles spun all around them. A few moments later, they were floating over Fairyland.

As they fluttered above emerald-green hills, Kirsty became curious about the birthday charms they were looking for and Belle explained. "The birthday book contains everyone's birthday. Without it, nobody knows when anyone's birthdays are!"

The girls nodded as Belle went on. "The magic birthday candle makes all birthday cakes delicious and grants wishes. The birthday present makes sure everyone receives the perfect gift."

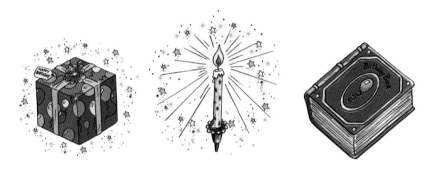

"Without those charms, nobody will ever have a happy birthday again!" said Rachel. She looked very glum.

"That's why Jack Frost stole them!" cried Belle. "It's his birthday soon, and he's feeling really miserable about his age and wants everyone else to be miserable too!"

"How mean!" said Kirsty.

As the three of them flew over the glittering turrets of the Fairyland Palace, Kirsty saw something. "Look!" she exclaimed.

Far below they could see three goblins scrambling up a ladder and into the palace!

"They're up to some mischief!" said Belle.

"Let's see if we can find out what's going on!"

Belle and the girls zoomed through the back door of the palace. Turning a corner, they watched as the goblins tiptoed into the library.

"What if this has something to do with the birthday charms?" whispered Rachel. "Let's creep in and listen to what they're saying."

The fairies fluttered silently into the cosy library.

"Look!" whispered Rachel as they ducked behind an armchair. The goblins were pulling books out and throwing them on the floor.

"Hurry up!" a tall goblin hissed. "We need to know when Jack Frost's birthday is so we can plan his surprise party!"

The girls stared at each other. The birthday book was hidden here in the Palace Library!

"The goblins want the book as much as we do," Kirsty realised. "Let's try and persuade them to help us!" She got up.

"We overheard what you said about the party," Kirsty began bravely. "You need that book as much as we do." The goblins whirled around in surprise.

"We'll let you stay and look up Jack Frost's birthday, if you promise to return the book to Belle," added Rachel.

The frowning goblins huddled together and, after lots of muffled arguing, they agreed.

The search went on and on, while outside the library the sun began to set.

At last, when every shelf had been searched from top to bottom, they pulled the cushions off the chairs. And there it was!

"I've got it!" yelled the smallest goblin.

The little goblin waved the shimmering book above his head, but it flew magically out of his hands and landed safely in Belle's arms.

As Belle turned the pages of the birthday book, the goblins spotted Jack Frost's name. They found his birthday on the list and scurried off.

"Thanks for helping me find this!" said Belle to the girls. "But it's time you two returned to the human world."

Belle smiled as she flicked her magic wand.

There was a whoosh of rainbow-coloured sparkles. When Kirsty and Rachel opened their eyes again they were back in the human world.

"I can't wait for our next fairy adventure!" smiled Kirsty.

The Birthday Candle

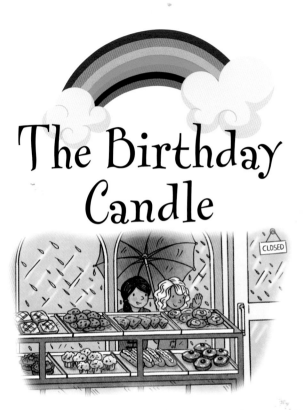

"I hope it stops raining before Mum's surprise party on Saturday," said Rachel. She and Kirsty were at the bakery to collect Mrs Walker's birthday cake. They were looking at the yummy treats in the window.

Inside the bakery, delicious smells filled the air.

"We've come to get the cake for Mrs Walker,"

Rachel said to the baker behind the counter.

"Oh dear," he replied sadly. "I'm having terrible trouble with that cake." Behind him, the girls could see what he meant. There sat a wonky cake with icing sliding off and sticky decorations lying beside it.

Suddenly, Kirsty tugged on Rachel's arm. "We have to go. We'll come back tomorrow," she said to the baker, as they walked out of the shop.

"Why do we have to leave so quickly?" asked Rachel, surprised.

"Because of what I've just seen at the window!" Kirsty whispered urgently.

Back outside, Kirsty pointed at three people who were crowding under one small umbrella. All three of them were wearing wellies. But Rachel looked again when she realised that above the wellies, she could see green legs!

"They're goblins!" she gasped. The girls stared in amazement at the silly green creatures. The goblins scurried into the bakery, splashing rainwater everywhere.

"I don't know what they're doing here," said Kirsty, "but we're getting soaked!"

And as Kirsty raised her umbrella above their heads, it began to glow inside like a glitter ball!

"Belle!" smiled Kirsty as the tiny fairy spiralled down the handle. "Thank goodness you're here! Three goblins have just gone into the bakery."

"I know," said Belle, unhappily. "I'm sure they're planning some mischief."

"We came to collect Mum's cake," said Rachel, "but it's all wonky."

Belle sighed. "No birthday cakes will bake properly until we find the missing candle charm."

"Belle, could you turn us into fairies?" asked Kirsty. "We simply must find out what those goblins are up to."

With a wave of Belle's wand and a flurry of sparkles, the girls shrank to fairy-size.

The bakery door was ajar, so the three fairies slipped inside and watched as the baker brought out cake after cake to show the goblins.

"These just aren't good enough!" said the tallest one, a mean look on his face.

"Boring!" shouted the middle goblin, poking a bony finger into a cake.

"But this is my best selection!" cried the baker.

"Ha!" snorted the tallest goblin. "We're from the Cake Standards Board, and we'll shut this bakery down unless you start making better ones!"

"We could make better cakes than this standing on our heads!" yelled the middle goblin.

"Get out!" screeched the smallest goblin, sneering at the confused baker.

"Go! Go! GO!" added the middle goblin. He gave the baker an umbrella and pushed him towards the door.

"I suppose I could take my lunch break now."
The poor baker watched as the goblins locked
the door behind him.

"Why are they being so horrible?" asked Rachel.

"I don't know," said Belle. "Let's find out!"
She flew after the goblins as they disappeared
into the kitchen at the back of the shop.

The goblins were
running around the
kitchen, spilling flour
and breaking eggs on
each other.

"Oh, no!" Kirsty
exclaimed. "They're
wrecking the place!"

"I think they're
trying to make a cake!"

said Belle, as they watched the goblins stir
ingredients in a mixing bowl.

"Stop shoving me!" squawked one of the
goblins, as he broke an egg over another's head.

"Shut up and fetch the candle!" the tallest
goblin snapped. The middle one stomped over
to the pile of coats and pulled a beautiful
shimmering cake candle out of one of the pockets.

"That's it!" said
Belle. "That's my
birthday candle
charm!"

The goblins
were still
crashing
around the
kitchen.

Just then, Rachel saw the one holding the candle add a large spoonful of chilli powder to the bowl.

"That's going to taste horrible!" she whispered.

At last, the goblin put the candle down on the worktop. He turned to put his cake into the oven. Rachel gulped, then flew down and grabbed the candle, just as the goblin turned back again!

"It's one of those pesky fairies!" he cried, grabbing a sieve and bringing it crashing down on top of Rachel. She was trapped!

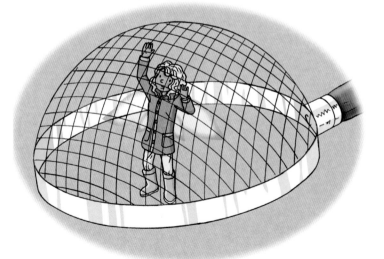

"Goblins, give me the candle and let Rachel go!" insisted Belle, swooping down.

"Shan't!" snapped the tallest goblin.

"Does Jack Frost know that you're here?" Kirsty asked the goblins.

They pale green. "No, we want his birthday cake to be a surprise!" said the smallest goblin in a trembling voice.

So that's what they were doing! thought Kirsty. "Without magic," she explained, "your cake will take hours to cook. And the baker will be back soon. If you help US, Belle can speed everything up a bit to help YOU!"

The goblins pulled faces at each other before nodding in agreement.

Belle waved her wand and the finished cake floated out of the oven. It landed safely on the table.

"It's horrible!" gasped Kirsty.

"It's spectacular!" grinned the goblins.

The cake was grey, ugly and misshapen. Perfect for Jack Frost.

The middle goblin lifted the sieve,

and Rachel made her escape. Belle flew down and picked up the birthday candle. She waved her wand over the cake. In a sparkle of magic it was transformed into Jack Frost's face, and topped with large candles. The goblins grabbed it, without bothering to say thank you, and rushed out of the door.

Belle flicked her wand, and the whole room shimmered. When the sparkles faded, the kitchen gleamed. A cake decorated with pink icing and pink hearts was sitting on the worktop.

"Perfect!" Rachel cried.

Outside, Belle returned Rachel and Kirsty to their human size. "Thanks to you two, birthday cakes and wishes are safe!" she said.

Belle disappeared in a flurry of fairy dust, clutching the precious birthday candle.

"I hope we can find the last missing birthday charm before Mum's party!" said Rachel.

"I just know we can!" Kirsty grinned.

The Birthday Present

"Surprise!" everyone shouted.

Balloons flew into the air and party poppers rained colourful streamers over the astonished Mrs Walker.

"What a wonderful surprise!" She smiled,

as all the guests wished her a happy birthday.

"Everything's going really well," Kirsty said in a low voice. "I was afraid that Jack Frost would spoil it because he's still got Belle's birthday present charm."

"That reminds me – it's time to give Mum her special gift!" said Rachel in excitement. "It's a jewellery box. I can't wait to see her face when she opens it!"

The two girls and Mr Walker handed the gift to Mrs Walker, who carefully undid the wrapping paper.

"Oh," she exclaimed, her face falling, as instead of a beautiful jewellery box, she found a pair of muddy old boots inside.

"It's not fair!" Rachel whispered to Kirsty. "Mum would have loved that jewellery box!" Beckoning Kirsty to follow her, she hurried outside and put her hand on the magical locket around her neck. The king and queen of Fairyland had given a locket full of fairy dust to each of the girls. They could use them to go to Fairyland in an emergency.

"We must help Belle find her birthday present charm!" Rachel said.

They sprinkled sparkling dust from their lockets over their heads. A glittering whirl tumbled them through the air towards Fairyland.

The fairy-sized girls found themselves inside the Fairyland Palace. It didn't take long to find Belle and describe what had happened at the party. Belle sighed and led them to the king and queen. They explained that all the preparations for Jack Frost's own party were going wrong.

All because he had hidden the birthday present somewhere in his Ice Castle!

"We could go to the Ice Castle and hunt for it!" Rachel offered at once.

"We want to help!" Kirsty agreed.

"Belle can go with you, but watch out," warned King Oberon. "It could be very dangerous."

The three fairies gazed up at Jack Frost's gleaming, icy home, wondering how they were ever going to get inside. Goblin guards were everywhere.

"Look!" cried Kirsty as she spied a goblin zooming towards the castle on a motorbike pulling a trailer. Quick as a flash, Belle, Rachel and Kirsty hid themselves in the trailer. They rumbled along the icy road until the engine was turned off. Then they heard the goblin walking away. They had made it!

The three brave fairies fluttered out and along a cold, gloomy corridor until they reached a door with "Great Hall" carved above it.

The girls darted into the hall and began their frantic search under tablecloths and behind curtains. But there were no presents, only cobwebs and woodlice!

Jack Frost's magnificent ice throne stood on a platform in the centre of the room. Eventually, Rachel saw there was a space underneath it.

It was full of beautifully wrapped gifts! They pulled them out one by one until Rachel found a tiny box, wrapped in pink paper.

"It's much sparklier than the others," she said.

"That's because it's my birthday present charm!" whispered Belle, her eyes shining with excitement.

Suddenly, the girls heard babbling goblin voices.

"Quick!" cried Kirsty. "Let's get back to the Fairyland Palace!"

Straightaway, Belle waved her wand, but nothing happened.

"Jack Frost must have put a spell on the room," she explained. "My magic doesn't work. And if we can't return the birthday present to the Fairyland Palace, the goblins' party preparations won't work either!"

Rachel gazed up at the windows. One of them was wide open.

Belle saw what Rachel was thinking. "We can't fly out of there," she whispered. "The goblins would grab us."

"They would – but not if they're distracted," replied Rachel with a smile.

Belle looked worried but there was no other way to return the birthday present.

"Hey, goblins! Over here!" shouted Kirsty.

The silly green creatures howled with anger and chased the fairies. None of them saw Belle slip out of the window.

Rachel and Kirsty flitted around the hall, dodging the goblins' grabbing hands. One jumped onto another's shoulders and tried to grab Rachel. But she did a somersault in mid-air. The goblin lost his balance and crashed to the floor with a yell.

"WHAT IS GOING ON?" roared Jack Frost from the doorway of the Great Hall. He looked at the chaos all around.

"The goblins are trying to throw you a birthday party," said the gentle voice of Queen Titania. She had arrived just in time.

With a wave of the queen's wand, the Great Hall was transformed into a party scene. The surprised Jack Frost was even more shocked when three goblins singing "Happy Birthday" carried in the cake with a picture of his face on!

It was the best party ever held at the Ice Castle. As night fell, Queen Titania beckoned to Rachel and Kirsty.

"You helped us show Jack that birthdays can be fun," said the queen. "But now, you have another party to attend!"

Belle hugged Rachel and Kirsty goodbye as a whirl of glittering fairy dust surrounded them. When the sparkles faded, they were back at Tippington Village Hall. They were just in time to see Mrs Walker opening her beautiful jewellery box.

"It's the perfect present!" said Kirsty.

"But no gift could be better than the adventure we've just had!" Rachel smiled.

Selena the Sleepover Fairy

The Fairyland Palace

Service Station

← Coach

Jack Frost's
Ice
Castle

National
Museum

NATIONAL MUSEUM

The Magical Sleeping Bag

"I can't believe we're going to a sleepover in the National Museum!" said Rachel Walker to her best friend Kirsty Tate as the coach rumbled down the motorway. "I can't wait. It's going to be so cool!"

The two best friends were among thirty children taking part in a schools' sleepover and everyone was super excited. After a while, the coach began to slow down.

"We'll stop here for twenty minutes," began Mr Ferguson, one of the teachers in charge. "So keep an eye on your watches." The service station was hidden from the motorway by a line of trees. As Rachel looked at them, something sparkled among the leaves.

"That looks like fairy dust!" she said. The girls were friends with the fairies, and often helped out when mischievous Jack Frost caused them trouble.

As the girls rushed towards the trees, glimmering purple sparkles whizzed around them, and suddenly a fairy appeared, carrying a teddy bear! "Hello," she said in a friendly, velvety voice. "I'm Selena the Sleepover Fairy."

Selena looked worried, and the two girls gasped as she gave them a warning. "Your sleepover could be at risk because Jack Frost has done something horrible!"

"What do you mean?" Kirsty asked, wide-eyed.

"Last night," explained Selena, "we held a fairy sleepover, but Jack Frost didn't like us having fun so he stole my three precious magical objects, and without them no sleepover will go smoothly."

"What are your magical objects?" Rachel asked the sad-looking fairy.

"The magical sleeping bag ensures that everyone gets a good night's sleep," Selena began. "Then there's the enchanted games bag,

which makes all games fun
and fair, and the sleepover
snack box guarantees
everyone will enjoy lots
of tasty food."

"We'll help you find
them," offered Rachel.

"And they may not be too far away!"
added Kirsty, pointing across to the car park.
They all turned to see six goblins climbing out
of the coach, carrying rucksacks and sleeping
bags. Jack Frost's goblin servants were clearly
up to something!

"Those naughty goblins!" exclaimed Kirsty.
As the girls watched, the green mischief-makers
scampered into the service station, laden down
with luggage.

Kirsty, Rachel and Selena, hidden in Kirsty's hair, hurried after them. The service station was so busy it was hard to see through the crowds but at last Rachel caught up with them. "That way!" she called. As the girls continued walking, they could hear squabbling goblin voices.

"Get off my sleeping bag!"

"Give it back!"

The goblins pushed against each other crossly,

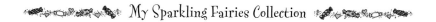

until one of them staggered into a magazine stand and knocked it over.

The silly goblins quickly ran off, and this time the girls couldn't keep up with them. They searched everywhere, eventually exploring right at the back of the service station. The lights weren't working and it was very quiet until suddenly they heard a giggle, and tiptoed around a corner. The goblins were all there, settling down inside their stolen sleeping bags. They were having a sleepover of their own!

One silly goblin had a sleeping bag that really didn't suit him. It was pink, decorated with hearts and sweets, and was glowing softly.

"That's my sleeping bag!" said a delighted Selena in a whisper.

Rachel and Kirsty stared at the sleeping bag.

"We can't get it back while there's a goblin inside it!" Rachel whispered.

"I've got an idea," said Kirsty, turning to Selena. "Could you perform a spell to make it really uncomfortable? Then he might get out!"

"Great idea," Selena smiled, waving her wand.

Suddenly the goblin wrinkled his nose. "Yuck! My sleeping bag stinks of strawberries," he complained, quickly clambering out of it.

Rachel and Kirsty ran towards the sleeping bag, but the goblins spotted them. They all jumped back in together, and zipped it up.

"Give that back!" exclaimed Rachel. But the silly, rude goblins just stuck out their tongues.

"All right," said Selena, waving her wand over the grinning goblins. "You stay there then."

Gradually, the goblins began to wriggle.

"It's very hot in here," said one.

"I can't undo the zip!" complained another. "That tricksy fairy has magicked it shut! We're stuck!"

"Now," began Selena. "Please give back the magical sleeping bag and everything else you took, and I'll give you your own sleeping bags."

Kirsty bit her lip anxiously.

"I'm too hot!" one goblin exclaimed. "I'll give it back – just let me out!"

"We agree!"

With a wave of her wand, the hot goblins tumbled out of the bag, and with a purple flash, each one had a stinky green sleeping bag under his arm.

"Can you magic them back to the Ice Castle?" Kirsty whispered to Selena.

"I can't," she sighed as they watched the goblins running to the car park and hiding on the coach with the luggage. "But I'll make sure they fall asleep and don't cause any mischief."

Selena magicked the sleeping bag back to fairy size, then sent all the ordinary sleeping bags and rucksacks safely back to the school coach.

Selena fluttered around in a whirl of violet sparkles. "I'll be back when I've returned the

magical sleeping bag to Fairyland," she smiled at the girls. "After all, we still have to find my other two magical objects!"

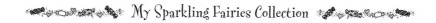

"We'll help!" Rachel promised with a big smile.

As the little fairy disappeared, Kirsty looked at her watch and gasped.

"Oh, no!" she said, grabbing Rachel's arm. "We've got to get back to the car park!"

They quickly ran towards the coach, climbed on board and dropped into their seats, panting and giggling.

"Just in time, girls!" smiled Mr Ferguson. "Next stop, the National Museum!"

The Enchanted Games Bag

As the coach rolled along, heading for the
museum, Rachel and Kirsty wondered if Selena
would be there to meet them. They couldn't wait
to see their fairy friend again.

When they arrived at the museum a bit later,

everyone eagerly filed off the coach. There
were bustling crowds of chattering, excited
children everywhere.

"Right, everybody," said Mr Ferguson.
"Take your things from the luggage hold and
line up in pairs."

"Oh, Kirsty!" Rachel exclaimed. "We have to
get to the luggage quickly and check that the
goblins aren't up to mischief!"

It seemed to take forever until the children in
front of them had collected their bags. At last it
was their turn.

"Here are our things," whispered Rachel, peering inside the luggage hold. "But there are no goblins."

"Selena's spell made the goblins go to sleep, but they must have got out when the bus stopped!" said Kirsty.

Everyone walked into the museum and, for the moment, the goblins were forgotten.

"Good evening," said a smiling lady.

"I'm Charlotte, and you are going to be in the Purple Group."

Rachel and Kirsty listened carefully as Charlotte told them about the treasure hunt.

"Each group must follow clues to find a letter of the alphabet," she explained. "When the letters are put together, they will spell out a place in the museum. That's where the midnight feast and storytelling will be held!"

Then Charlotte gave them each a purple cap.

"The enchanted games bag is missing," Kirsty whispered to Rachel as they dropped off their bags. "Without it, the treasure hunt will go wrong!"

They followed Charlotte to the Roman Gallery, where she handed an envelope to each pair of children.

"Good luck finding the letter!" she smiled.

Kirsty opened the envelope and read out their clue.

Harder than glass and richer than crowns, you'll find me on fingers and fabulous gowns!

"Diamonds are harder than glass," Kirsty whispered.

"But there are no diamonds here," said Rachel.

She frowned, looking around. "I think something's wrong with the clues."

"Look!" said Kirsty suddenly, pointing to a Roman vase nearby. It was glowing! Suddenly Selena zoomed out of it, and the girls crouched down, out of sight.

"I've seen the enchanted games bag!" gushed the tiny fairy. "A boy wearing a red cap has it."

"One of the goblins must have dropped it," said Rachel thoughfully. "And the boy picked it up."

Suddenly, they spotted someone short rushing past the door.

"A goblin!" cried Kirsty.

"Let's follow him!" said Rachel.

Selena waved her wand, and the girls were caught in a whirl of tiny sparkling stars as they shrank to fairy size.

They zoomed out of the gallery and glimpsed the goblin running down the main staircase. They flew closely behind him and when they reached the bottom, they saw six more goblins, messing around behind the desk!

Selena and the girls hid behind a dinosaur model and watched as the goblin they had been following rushed up to the desk.

"I can't find the pesky human child who picked up the fairy bag," he said.

"We'll all come and look," sighed another.

"We must find that boy before the goblins do!" said Selena in an urgent whisper.

The three fairies darted down a long corridor, peering closely at everyone. But nobody was carrying anything that looked magical. Rachel noticed a boy standing beside a dinosaur model.

He was carrying a bag, and as she watched, she noticed that it was glowing strongly.

"Look!" Selena said. "The enchanted games bag must be inside!"

But before they could decide what to do, a goblin leaned down from the dinosaur and dipped his hand into the unzipped bag.

Luckily, just then the boy strode out of the gallery, with goblins scurrying after him and the fairies fluttering above.

Next, the boy paused beside a model of a polar bear, and the girls watched as two goblins scrambled up its back.

Realising what they were going to do, Selena swept her wand over Rachel and Kirsty's heads to make them human size again.

"Girls," she whispered to Rachel and Kirsty,

who saw what was happening just in time and shouted to the boy, "Look out!"

The boy whipped around and the goblin landed on the ground with a furious squawk.

"Give me that bag NOW!" he demanded rudely. The boy looked angry.

"I found it, so it's finders keepers!" he retorted.

"Excuse me," said Rachel.

"Oh, hello," the boy said, turning to face them.

"Thank you for warning me."

"You're welcome," Kirsty replied. "You see, we've been looking for you too. I think you've got our friend's bag, and she needs it back."

The boy stared at them thoughtfully, and then looked at the green-hatted goblin sulking nearby. "This boy's been trying to take it from me too. It must be very special."

"It is," said Kirsty gently.

The boy reached into his travel bag, and drew out the games bag. Smiling broadly, he held it out to Rachel. The goblin snorted with rage.

As the boy said goodbye and headed back to find his group, Selena hovered in front of the girls. With a flick of her wand, the enchanted games bag returned to fairy size, and she smiled at Rachel and Kirsty.

"Thank you for persuading him to give back the magic bag," she said.

"You're welcome," replied Rachel. "Are you taking it back to Fairyland?"

"Yes," Selena said. "But I'll be back. We still have the sleepover snack box to find!"

As the little fairy disappeared in a flurry of pinky-purple dust, Rachel and Kirsty wandered back to the Roman Gallery.

When they arrived, Mr Ferguson was looking very pleased about something.

"Charlotte has found some brand-new sets of clues," he told them. Now that everything was back to normal, the groups set off on their treasure hunts again. Altogether they found five letters.

Everyone gathered in the entrance hall and studied the letters together. "Who will be the first to put the letters in the right order?" Charlotte asked.

"It spells 'crypt'," called out the boy who had found the enchanted games bag.

"Correct," said Charlotte, sounding impressed.

Rachel and Kirsty looked at each other. A midnight feast in a crypt? How exciting!

The Sleepover Snack Box

Charlotte handed each of the children a glass lantern. "It's dark in the crypt," she smiled. There were lots of gasps and giggles and they followed Charlotte down a long, winding staircase.

It grew colder and darker as they travelled
deeper underground. At last they reached an old,
wooden door. Charlotte pushed it open, it gave
a loud *CREEEAAAKK!* and they faced a long,
dark passageway.

"This is where we keep all the exhibits that aren't being used," Charlotte said. In the dim light from their lanterns, the girls saw mysterious boxes and tall vases. There were lots of strange shapes covered in white sheets. The long snake of children wound through more dusty passages until they found themselves in a big room.

There was a man sitting down, smiling, on an ornate chair.

"This is Zack the Storyteller," Charlotte explained to everyone. As the children moved towards him, Charlotte peered behind a curtain and Rachel and Kirsty caught a glimpse of a long, empty wooden table. Charlotte looked worried as she hurried over to Zack. "There's a bit of a problem," they heard her say. "The feast isn't ready. Could you start the story while I go and sort it out?"

"This must be because the sleepover snack box is still missing!" whispered Rachel.

"Welcome to the crypt," said Zack.

Rachel started listening to the story, but Kirsty was distracted. She kept thinking that someone was behind her. Eventually she turned her head, and saw a spiky-headed shadow!

She quickly nudged Rachel, but before she could turn around to look, the strange shadow had completely disappeared.

"Maybe it was the lantern light making funny shapes on the wall?" Rachel suggested. Looking at her own lantern, she gasped. It was shining very brightly, and suddenly Selena the Sleepover Fairy shot out!

"I have news!" she said. "Jack Frost is so fed up with the silly goblins losing everything, he's taken the sleepover snack box himself!"

"I think he's here!" whispered Kirsty. "I just saw his shadow."

"He's searching for the goblins!" Selena realised.

"We have to find him!" whispered Rachel urgently, looking worried.

"And the sleepover snack box!" added Kirsty.

The girls looked around. Zack was well into his story now, and everyone's attention was on him. They crept after Selena into a far corner, and the fairy waved her tiny wand. There was a faint musical sound, and the girls shrank to fairy size, along with their bright lanterns.

"We must look like tiny fireflies!" giggled Rachel as they rose up into the air.

Flying close together, the three friends made their way down a long, dark passage.

Suddenly, they heard a crash and a loud squawk.

"It sounded like a goblin!" cried Selena.

As the fairies' eyes got used to the light, they saw a pile of boxes had toppled onto two goblins.

One was rubbing a large red bump on his head. The other was rubbing his foot.

"Shhh!" said a third goblin. "Do you want Jack Frost to hear us?"

"You said there was going to be a wonderful feast, but it's cold and dark, and I'm hungry,"

grumbled the first goblin angrily.

"Come on," whispered Selena. "Jack Frost's not here. Let's look somewhere else."

They flew back along the tunnel and out into the main room. Suddenly, Rachel gave a cry. "Look!" she whispered, pointing.

Jack Frost was quietly skulking in the shadows, carrying the sleepover snack box under his arm!

"We have to get him away from the other children," said Kirsty. "They would be really scared if they spotted him!"

"Why is he just standing there?" asked Selena.

"I think he wants to hear Zack's story!" said Rachel.

"I've got an idea," said Kirsty to Selena. "Could you use your magic to make our voices sound like goblins? Then Jack Frost might follow us."

Selena waved her wand, and the girls swooped down.

"Silly old Jack Frost!" said Rachel, giggling like a goblin.

Jack Frost's head whipped around, but of course, he couldn't see any goblins.

The girls zoomed into the tunnel entrance.

"Over here!" teased Kirsty, waving her arms

in the air, just as Zack reached a very spooky part of his story.

The light from Rachel's lantern cast Kirsty's shadow onto the wall, making it look huge and monstrous.

Jack Frost gave a cry, dropped the box and ran away! His terrified scream was so loud, the goblins heard it and thought it was a ghost. They scampered out of the tunnel after him.

"Thank goodness!" said Rachel with a smile.

"Jack Frost and the goblins have gone, and we've found the sleepover snack box."

"You've both been wonderful, girls!" said Selena, hugging them tightly. "I am so happy to

have all my magical objects back where they belong!"

Selena transformed the sleepover snack box to its Fairyland size with a touch of her sparkly wand. Kirsty and Rachel gave her a big smile. Then the fairy made the two girls human size again.

"It's nice to have my own voice back!" laughed Kirsty.

"Goodbye, and thank you," said Selena with a beaming smile. The air filled with fairy dust, and Selena was gone.

The girls slipped back into the hall just as the story ended and Charlotte appeared with trays of delicious-smelling food. There were bowls of yummy strawberries and masses of iced cupcakes.

After the feast, Charlotte announced it was time for bed. But there were groans from everyone.

"... after a game of hide-and-seek, of course!" Charlotte said with a laugh.

"I'm glad we found all the magical objects in time," Rachel said. "Now we can enjoy the rest of the sleepover! It's the perfect end to a truly magical adventure!"

Shannon the Ocean Fairy

The
Fairyland
Palace

Hawaiian Island

Surfing Waves

Dolphins

Baby Seahorses

← Coral

The Enchanted Pearl

Rachel Walker and her best friend Kirsty Tate raced
across Leamouth Beach, laughing. They were on
holiday together, staying with Kirsty's gran.

Down where the waves lapped onto the
sand, the girls noticed a beautiful seashell.

They gasped as a burst of pale blue sparkles fizzed out of it.

"Fairy magic!" Kirsty whispered. Their friendship with the fairies was a very special secret.

"Hello, girls," said a voice from the shell.

"It's the Fairy Queen!" Rachel grinned.

"We'd like to invite you to a special beach party," said the queen. "I hope you can come."

Suddenly, a rainbow shot out from the shell.
When the two friends stepped onto it, they
disappeared in a whirl of fairy magic.

The girls had been magically turned into
fairies and were now standing on a different
beach. It was crowded with fairies enjoying
a party. King Oberon and Queen Titania
welcomed them.

"The tide's coming in. Will the party end soon?"
Rachel asked
a nearby
fairy. It was
Shannon the
Ocean Fairy!
She was
wearing a
pink skirt,

and had a glittering starfish clip in her hair.

"No. The sea never comes beyond Party Rock," Shannon smiled, pointing to a large boulder.

Suddenly, the party music stopped.

"The sea's coming in too far!" called Shannon. "Something's wrong!"

"Jack Frost must be up to mischief again," said King Oberon. He asked Shannon to dive into the waves and look for clues in her underwater world.

Just then, a frog footman arrived. He told the king and queen that Jack Frost and his goblins had stolen the three Enchanted Pearls. Jack Frost hadn't been invited to the party, so he was determined to ruin it for everyone else.

Rachel and Kirsty exchanged an excited look. Whenever Jack Frost caused trouble in Fairyland, the girls helped the fairies put things right.

When Shannon the Ocean Fairy came fluttering back, King Oberon explained that Jack Frost had taken the pearls.

"My underwater world is in chaos!" Shannon cried sadly.

Kirsty and Rachel looked confused, so the little fairy started to explain.

"The Dawn Pearl makes sure that dawn comes every single morning. It also affects the amount of water in the oceans. The Twilight Pearl makes sure that night falls every evening. The Moon Pearl controls the size of the waves."

"We'll help you find them!" said Rachel, eager to help.

Shannon grinned at them and raised her wand. As magic sparkles whizzed around them,

Rachel and Kirsty shut their eyes. They opened them a moment later to find themselves standing on the sandy seabed.

"We're under the sea!" Kirsty cried.

"It's magical!" Rachel laughed as she realised she was breathing and talking as if she was on land.

Shannon swam off. The two girls followed,

whizzing through the water past colourful fish and coral caves. They were looking for clues. A moment later, three goblins swam towards them. One goblin was carrying a large rosy-pink pearl!

Rachel and Kirsty gazed at the pearl. It shone with a brightness that filled the ocean with light. At that moment, the goblins shot forward, holding the pearl like a torch.

"There's no treasure here!" the biggest one said to the others in disgust. They moved along the seabed, pearly light shining all around.

"Oh, no!" Shannon cried suddenly. She peered through a small opening in the nearby rock wall.

Rachel and Kirsty looked puzzled.

"This is the Mermaid Kingdom," Shannon whispered. "Mermaids are very secretive and would hate their kingdom to be revealed!"

"Maybe we can tempt the goblins away with some treasure!" Kirsty suggested. "If you could magic up some gold coins, we could lay a trail."

"Good idea," said Shannon. "With the goblins trapped, maybe we can get the Dawn Pearl back." She waved her wand and a trail of shiny coins appeared in the sand, leading to a nearby coral cave.

Before long, the goblins came past. "Treasure!" yelled one of them, spotting a glinting coin.

Shannon, Rachel and Kirsty swam silently after the goblins as they picked up the coins one by one.

"Let's go!" Shannon whispered. The goblins shrieked with surprise when they saw the three fairies at the cave entrance.

"Please give me the Dawn Pearl," Shannon said politely.

"No way!" said one of the goblins. "You silly
fairies can't make us!"

Just as the girls were wondering what to do,
they saw lots of lobsters snapping at the goblins'
ankles. The scared goblins backed away.

"Maybe we can't, but my lobster friends can!"

Shannon smiled. "And they'll snap at your ears and noses too."

"It's yours," the biggest of the goblins squeaked, tossing the Dawn Pearl to Shannon.

"Thank you," Shannon called. "And thank you, my lobster friends!" She waved her wand. In a burst of shimmering fairy dust, Shannon, Rachel and Kirsty were back on the empty beach in Leamouth.

Then the little fairy used her magic to make the girls human size again.

"I must take the Dawn Pearl back to Fairyland now," Shannon said. "Thank you for all your help. Don't forget, we still have the other two Enchanted Pearls to find!"

Rachel and Kirsty nodded and smiled as Shannon disappeared with the pearl in a whirl of sparkling fairy magic.

Trouble at Sea

The next morning, Rachel, Kirsty and Gran were walking along the seafront. "You explore," Gran said. "But be quick – a storm's on the way."

The two girls headed off along the pier. The sky was getting darker and darker even though the sun was shining. Kirsty and Rachel were just passing a games arcade, when a machine began flashing.

"FREE PLAY," Rachel read aloud from the little screen.

The machine was full of soft toys. A metal claw hung above them. The claw, used to grab the toys, was operated by a lever. Rachel held the lever and moved the claw around, finally managing to grab a fluffy dolphin.

"Well done!" Kirsty cried.

Smiling, Rachel collected her prize from the machine. She gasped as a beautiful cloud of yellow sparkles burst out.

"Hello, girls!" Shannon the Ocean Fairy cried. "I need your help to find the Twilight Pearl. Now, quick, get out of sight!"

Rachel and
Kirsty were
very keen
to help.
They ducked
behind the
machine,
where
Shannon
flicked
her wand,

transforming them into fluttering fairies. As they flew off the end of the pier, Shannon explained how nightfall was being disrupted everywhere. All because the Twilight Pearl was missing!

"Where are the goblins with the Twilight Pearl?" Kirsty asked.

"I think they're underwater. Near here," said Shannon. "That's why it's so dark by the pier."

Then the little fairy tapped her wand until the tip began to sparkle brightly. "We'll use this to light our way under the sea and my fairy magic will help you breathe underwater," she said to the girls.

Suddenly, Shannon plunged into the sparkling blue ocean. Rachel and Kirsty followed.

"This way," Shannon said, darting through the water. It was becoming darker and darker.

Kirsty wondered how they were ever going to find the goblins. Even with Shannon's glowing wand, it was hard to see anything in the dark water.

"Wait here!" Shannon called. She swam off. Seconds later she returned with a school of beautiful dolphins behind her!

"The dolphins know the ocean better than anyone," Shannon explained. "Jump on, girls, and hold tight. They're going to take us to the goblins." The excited girls clung on tightly as the dolphins zipped through the darkening sea.

After a while the dolphins slowed down. The girls could hear voices ahead.

"Goblins!" whispered Kirsty.

"I don't like the dark," one goblin whimpered. "I can't see!"

"Help!" the goblins called.

As the light from Shannon's wand shone through the black water, the goblins sneered at them.

"Give the Twilight Pearl back and we'll rescue you," Shannon offered.

"We're not scared!" The biggest goblin shivered.

"OK then. We'll go now, and take our light with us," Shannon said firmly.

"NO! Please stay," sobbed the goblin. "But we can't give the pearl back because we've hidden it and now we can't find it!"

"We know it's under a really big rock," said another goblin. They all looked sadly at the hundreds of big rocks around them.

Just then, Kirsty had a brilliant idea.

"There's an old lighthouse by the pier.
Could your magic get it working again?" she
asked Shannon.

"Maybe," the little fairy replied. "Stay here!"
she told the goblins, as the three fairies shot up
into the sky.

"There's the lighthouse!" Rachel cried. They
flew in through a broken window under the roof.

Shannon pointed her wand at the huge broken lantern. Slowly, it lit up and began to turn.

"It's lighting up the sea," Kirsty cheered.

"Look!" Rachel called. She pointed at a silver shimmer in the water.

"The Twilight Pearl!" Shannon exclaimed. The little fairy whizzed out of the lighthouse, and dived into the glittering patch of sea.

Rachel and Kirsty followed her.

The pearl lay beneath a large rock. But as they all gazed at its magical sheen,

a goblin swam past and grabbed it!

Luckily, Shannon knew exactly what to do.

"If you don't give that magical pearl back," the fairy called after him, "I'll turn the lighthouse off and leave you here in the dark."

The goblin was scared.

"Fine!" he yelled. "Take it, you horrible fairies!" He stuck his tongue out at them, and swam away crossly.

"Everyone in Fairyland will be so pleased to have the Twilight Pearl returned," Shannon said to Rachel and Kirsty. "But you must get back to Leamouth."

The three friends flew quickly to the deserted end of the pier. Shannon used some magic to make Kirsty and Rachel human size again.

"We just have the Moon Pearl to find now," Shannon reminded the girls. She gave them a big hug and disappeared in a cloud of fairy dust.

"I wonder where the goblins have hidden the Moon Pearl," Rachel said to Kirsty as they waved goodbye.

"I don't know, but I can't wait to find out!" replied Kirsty with a smile.

Pearl Power

The next day, Kirsty's gran was reading the newspaper.

"Oh, dear!" she said suddenly.

"What's the matter, Gran?" asked Kirsty. She and Rachel were busy packing their bags for a trip to the beach.

"There are lots of floods all over the world,"

Gran explained. "The sea is behaving very strangely."

Rachel and Kirsty looked worried. They knew it was because the Moon Pearl, which looked after the tides, was missing from Fairyland.

"Have fun, but make sure you're back in time for lunch," called Gran, as the girls hurried through the garden towards the beach. "And watch out for the tides!"

"I wonder if Shannon has found out where the goblins are hiding the Moon Pearl," said Rachel.

The girls had arrived on the empty beach. It was still very early so there weren't many people about. They were paddling in the clear water when Rachel spotted a glass bottle bobbing on the waves.

"Look," she said, grabbing it. "There's a piece of paper in it saying 'Open me!'"

As Kirsty pulled out the cork, Shannon the Ocean Fairy burst out of the bottle, along with a sparkling mist of sea-green bubbles!

"I need your help!" Shannon said quickly. "Fairyland is flooding, so we must find the Moon Pearl! I think it's at Breezy Bay Beach, with the naughty goblins."

"But how do we get there?" asked Kirsty.

"With fairy magic, of course!" Shannon smiled. She waved her wand and turned the girls into fairies.

"Follow me," she said, diving into the waves.

The three friends were carried through the ocean by a magical current. They whizzed through the clear water past colourful fish and coral reefs. Slowing down, they swam to the surface and popped out of the sea onto a beach.

Suddenly, Rachel, Kirsty and Shannon could hear shouting and laughter. They turned to see a big wave heading towards the beach. A group of goblins was riding the wave on big, colourful surfboards.

"They look so funny!" Rachel whispered, giggling. "But aren't they supposed to be hiding with the Moon Pearl?"

"I think they've forgotten about that!"
Shannon grinned.

"The waves are enormous!" Kirsty gasped.

"Breezy Bay is famous for its big waves,"
Shannon said. "But I think the goblins are using
the Moon Pearl to make the waves even bigger
than usual."

"Then let's start searching!" Kirsty said eagerly.

The three friends ducked under the water again. They spotted a group of blue seahorses bobbing towards them. Shannon explained that they were friends of hers.

"We're looking for the Moon Pearl," she told the smiling creatures. "Have you seen it?"

The seahorses all bounced up and down, looking very excited.

"We think so!" explained one in a tiny voice.
"Not far from here are two strange green
creatures with flappy feet."

"And they're guarding a big white pearl,"
added another.

"Over there, over there!" chorused the rest.

"Thank you," Shannon said with a smile.
"Come on, girls."

They swam off quickly. Before long, they
spotted two goblins playing catch with a big,

creamy-white pearl. Darting behind a rock, the fairies worked out what to do.

"There are only two of them," Shannon whispered. "This is our chance!"

"Let's sneak over and grab the pearl when it's in mid-air," Rachel suggested.

"Great idea!" Kirsty agreed.

When the goblin tossed the pearl, Rachel swam forwards, stretching her arms to grab it.

But it was just too high for her to catch!

"It's those annoying fairies!" yelled one goblin. The other goblin zoomed over and snatched the pearl away from Rachel's fingers. They shot off, using their huge flappy feet to help them go faster.

"After them!" Shannon cried.

But the goblins were getting away.

"They're too fast," Shannon panted. "It's no good." She stopped and looked dismayed.

"How are we ever going to get the Moon Pearl back?"

Just then, they heard a chorus of tiny voices say, "We can help! We can help!"

The friendly little seahorses were back!

"Jump on our backs," the seahorses called, "and hold on tight!"

"They're fast!" Kirsty gasped, clinging onto her seahorse's neck as they zoomed away.

"There are the goblins," Rachel said, spotting them. "But how will we get the pearl?"

As they whizzed past a clump of seaweed, Kirsty had an idea.

"We could tie the goblins up!" she suggested.

"Good idea," said Shannon. With a burst of magic, she knotted together some seaweed.

Quietly, the fairies and their seahorses sneaked up behind the goblins. Holding the long string of seaweed, they whizzed round and round the goblins.

"Help!" shrieked the goblins as the seaweed rope tightened around them.

Shannon took the Moon Pearl from their hands. "While you are freeing yourselves," she scolded, "think about how naughty you've been!"

After thanking the seahorses, Shannon

showered herself and the girls with magic
sparkles. Suddenly, they were back in the air,
flying over Fairyland.

"Look at the water!" Rachel gasped. Many of
the toadstool houses were flooded.

Shannon swooped swiftly in through an
open window of the Fairyland Palace and
returned the Moon Pearl to its proper place.

Almost at once, the water began to disappear.

"Thank you for your help," said Shannon to the girls. She pointed her wand and a shower of fairy dust fell around them. When it cleared, they gasped with delight. They were each wearing a gold ring with a rosy pink pearl in the centre.

"They're beautiful!" said the girls together.

"Now, you should get back to Gran's," said Shannon. She waved her wand and a few seconds later, the girls were human size and back on Leamouth Beach.

"What an amazing adventure!" Kirsty cheered. "This really has been the best holiday ever!"

Keira the Film Star Fairy

The Fairyland
Palace

Meadow

Trailers

Stepping
Stones

Village

SHOP

The Silver Script

"Look, there's Julianna Stewart!" whispered Kirsty Tate, spying the film star reading her script.

"Who would have thought a famous actress would come here to Wetherbury Village?" said her best friend, Rachel Walker.

Julianna Stewart was starring in a movie called *The Starlight Chronicles*, and it was being filmed in

Mrs Croft's garden! Someone from a film company had knocked on her door one day and asked if they could use her pretty cottage for the movie.

Mrs Croft was a friend of Kirsty's parents and had managed to get the girls parts as magical fairies – which was perfect for them! They had secretly visited Fairyland many times and were always ready to protect their fluttery friends from mean Jack Frost and his naughty goblin servants.

"I can't wait to try on our costumes!" grinned Kirsty. The film set bustled with people. Helpers known as runners fetched props, and dancers practised their steps. The girls watched as Julianna took her place in front of Chad Stenning, the actor playing the fairy prince.

"And . . . action!" cried the director.

Everyone watched as Chad gave a deep bow. "Please walk with me on the terrace. There is something I must say." He offered his arm to Julianna and led her off the set.

"Excellent!" announced the director.

"I haven't seen that runner before," said Rachel, nudging her friend. "He seems in a terrible hurry."

The runner rushed past the actors, then snatched a script from the director's table.

"That's not a runner," Kirsty said breathessly, spotting a patch of green skin. "It's a goblin!"

Rachel gasped as she caught sight of a pair of warty green feet.

The girls started to follow him just as the director called, "Action!"

Everyone waited for Julianna and Chad to start speaking. But they were totally silent.

At last Julianna spoke.

"My mind's gone blank!" she exclaimed.

"That's strange," whispered Rachel. "She's never forgotten her words before. Something – or someone – is upsetting things."

"We must find that goblin!" Kirsty replied.

Rachel led the way along a path of stepping stones that led to a meadow behind Mrs Croft's cottage. It was full of mobile homes in all shapes and sizes. The actors and crew

were staying here together during filming.

"That way!" cried Rachel, watching the goblin's baseball cap disappearing behind a plush-looking silver trailer.

Suddenly, a wardrobe mistress with a tape measure around her neck pushed a rail of fancy fairy outfits right across their path.

"Coming through!" she cried.

Kirsty sighed. "We'll never catch the goblin now. It'll be too late by the time we get past these costumes."

As the girls tried to step around the rail, tiny scarlet stars began to shimmer above a beautiful gown until suddenly,

a pretty fairy burst out from it, landing on the rail.

"Hi!" she smiled. "I'm Keira the Film Star Fairy."

"Hello!" grinned Kirsty and Rachel, following the fairy as she fluttered to a quiet part of the meadow.

"I look after movie-makers in Fairyland and the human world," she explained. "And I really need your help."

Kirsty and Rachel listened as Keira told them about her three precious magical objects.

"The silver script makes sure the actors get their lines right. The magical megaphone helps directors organise everyone and the enchanted clapperboard gets the camera rolling. Everything was fine," she sighed, "until Jack Frost decided he wanted to be a film star."

Keira told the girls how the Ice Lord had sent his goblins to snatch the silver script.

"If we don't find it," the little fairy went on, "Julianna and the others won't be able to perform properly!"

"We just saw a goblin steal a script!" cried Kirsty, as Keira fluttered into her jacket pocket.

"This way!" said the fairy, pointing her shimmering wand towards the woods.

Kirsty peeped through the trees. "I can see the goblin!" she gasped. "He's got the silver script, and he's not alone!"

"I have to be the director!" they heard a pointy-nosed goblin shout.

"Only if I can be the prince," snapped another.

Within moments they were tugging at the script and arguing.

"I've got an idea," whispered Rachel. "Keira, would you be able to magic us some smart clothes?"

"Of course!" replied Keira, waving her wand and transforming their outfits into

suits and dark glasses.

The girls stepped into the clearing.

"We're from Hollywood," Rachel announced. "And we thought you might like some tips."

A goblin with big ears shrugged his shoulders.

"Let's start with some acting exercises," began Rachel. "I'll give you a scene to act out."

"Shan't," yelled the goblin clutching the script.

"Oh," sighed Rachel. "But you've got the starring role!"

"I'll do it!" he cried suddenly.

"Just imagine," continued Rachel, "that you are a famous author. Now pretend you are coming to my office to deliver your new story."

"Are we ready?" cut in Kirsty suddenly. "Then . . . action!"

The goblin opened an imaginary door.

"I think you'll enjoy reading this," he began importantly, handing her the silver script.

Suddenly, Keira burst from Kirsty's pocket and tapped the silver script with her wand, shrinking it to fairy size.

"Thanks, Mr Goblin Writer!" she smiled.

The goblins squawked and leapt with rage.

"This is going back to Fairyland," she told them firmly. "Where it belongs."

When the silly goblins had run off to hide from Jack Frost, Keira smiled.

"Thank you," she said, magically changing the girls back into their normal clothes, and disappearing in a puff of fairy dust.

"Goodbye!" waved the girls.

"Let's go back to the film set," Kirsty suggested, linking arms with her best friend. "I'll bet those rehearsals are on track again!"

The Magical Megaphone

Back in Mrs Croft's garden, people scurried around everywhere. "Let's sit over there," suggested Rachel, pointing to a wooden bench. It was the perfect place to watch the rehearsal.

"Let's roll!" announced the director.

Everyone waited for Julianna to say her first line, but instead, she wandered over to Chad,

who was still having his
make-up done!

"Miss Stewart,"
began the director
gently. "The scene
with your fairy
servants under the
tree comes first. Then
you move across to
the prince."

Julianna frowned, looking very confused.

"Let's try again. Ladies-in-waiting, where are
you?" he bellowed.

"Over here," they waved from across the
garden. "Where you told us to be."

"That's not what I said!" he wailed.

"Something's wrong," said Kirsty worriedly.

"No one knows what they should be doing!"

"This is awful!" declared Rachel as they watched the director trying to sort out the muddle.

Suddenly, the fountain in front of them began to bubble higher, and there, rising on the crest of the cascade, was Keira! The little fairy's face was pale with worry as she beckoned them over to the bushes at the back of the garden.

"Will you come with me to Fairyland?" she gasped,

her eyes wide. "We haven't got much time!"

Keira explained that Queen Titania had made
a special request for Kirsty and Rachel's help.

"Of course we'll come!" cried both the girls
at once.

A whirl of fairy magic spun around the
friends as they felt themselves getting smaller
and smaller. Soon they were the same size as
Keira, with shimmering wings on both of their
shoulders. The three fairies joined hands and
closed their eyes. When they opened them again,

they were gliding above the emerald hills of
Fairyland. They landed in the pretty walled
garden of the Fairyland Palace. In the centre
was a pond, which Kirsty and Rachel recognised
as the magical Seeing Pool. Queen Titania was
standing next to it.

"Hello again, dear girls!" she said warmly.

"Your Majesty," said Rachel breathlessly.

The queen waved her wand over the Seeing Pool.

"Thank you for coming," she
said to them sadly. "*The
Starlight Chronicles* is
in serious trouble."

As the pool shone with
magical light, a picture of
Jack Frost slowly formed
on the surface.

"He's on the film set!" gasped Rachel.

As they watched, the Ice Lord picked up a megaphone and stuffed it under his cloak.

"And that's the magical megaphone!" cried Keira. "I'd lent it to *The Starlight Chronicles* to make sure filming went well. But now it's locked away in the Ice Castle!"

Suddenly Rachel and Kirsty realised why everything had been going wrong.

"Would you all go to Jack Frost's Ice Castle to find it?" Queen Titania asked the girls.

They nodded their heads. "Of course, Your Majesty," said Kirsty.

"Thank you, dear friends," said the queen,

lifting up her wand once again.

"The magical megaphone should be easy to find. Its sound can travel for miles."

Queen Titania pointed her wand up to the sky. Fairy dust sparkled and flashed all around the fairies, and when it settled, the beautiful palace gardens had disappeared. Instead they found

themselves in a dark wood. A wind blew through the icy trees, making all the fairies shiver.

"The Ice Castle is on the other side of this wood,"

whispered Keira, looking frightened.

Suddenly a chilly voice rang around the trees.

"You goblins are useless!" it cried.

"That's Jack Frost!" gasped Rachel, looking nervously around her.

"All you had to do was bring back the silver script!" the voice boomed.

The fairies flew through freezing clouds towards the Ice Castle. As they got closer, Jack Frost's angry shouts got louder and louder.

They landed in the courtyard, and the noise was terrible. Jack Frost was pacing around, shouting at the goblins through the magical megaphone!

The goblins were all wandering around with their fingers in their ears, bumping into each other in confusion and wailing at the horrible noise.

"Stop him!" Kirsty shouted over the din.

"I can't hear you!" Rachel frowned.

Luckily, Keira knew just what to do. She tapped her wand against her ear, and as golden stars surrounded them, the girls felt earplugs slip into their ears. In blissful silence, they looked around. One by one the stars touched the goblins, and earplugs slid into their ears too.

"Peace at last," Keira
mouthed to the girls.

Jack Frost was ordering
the goblins about,
but they just stared
gormlessly. They couldn't
hear a word he was saying!

"Hurry up! Get on with it!" Jack Frost
screamed, getting more and more furious.

"What's wrong with this thing?" he snarled,
shaking the megaphone and

peering inside it. Rachel
spotted her chance. As quick
as a flash, she darted inside
the other end and then
burst out, right into Jack
Frost's face!

"Aarrghh!" he yelled in shock, dropping the magical megaphone.

"That's mine!" cried Keira, zooming towards her precious possession. As soon as her hand touched it, it shrank down to fairy size.

Kirsty and Rachel followed Keira up into the air, taking care to flutter out of Jack Frost's reach.

"Pesky fairies!" he fumed. "Come back here or I'll set my goblins on you!" The meanie glared at his servants, but they simply grunted, shrugged and scratched their heads.

"They can't hear a word!" chuckled Keira, pulling her earplugs out. The girls did the same and then all three sets of earplugs magically disappeared.

"What a gormless bunch!" barked Jack Frost angrily, storming up and down the courtyard.

"Can't you lot do anything I tell you?"

"What's up with him?" sniffed one of the goblins, nudging a pal in the ribs. The other goblin gawped at his master then pulled a silly face. "Lucky we've got these earplugs in!" he sniggered.

"Time to go!" beamed Keira, waving her wand and holding on tight to her megaphone.

In a fizz of stars, she whisked them all away with Jack Frost's shouts still echoing in the distance.

After everyone had said goodbye, a sparkling shower of magic from Keira's wand turned Rachel and Kirsty back to human size again. Could this holiday get any more exciting?

The Enchanted Clapperboard

Kirsty and Rachel were both feeling very excited. It was finally time for them to play their parts as extras in *The Starlight Chronicles*! "I can't wait to show our costumes to Keira," whispered Kirsty.

Each girl was dressed in a pale pink gown,

and, with all the other extras, had spent the
morning having their hair and make-up done.
The first scene was to be filmed inside Mrs
Croft's pretty house. They would be attending the
fairy princess on the morning of her wedding.

"I hope I can remember where to stand!"
said an extra called Angel. Her friend, Emily,

anxiously bent
down to tie the
ribbons on her
satin slippers.

Suddenly,
the door
opened and there
were gasps as
Julianna stepped
onto the set.

"You look perfect!" exclaimed Rachel.

Large dazzling spotlights shone onto the sparkling set as the director held up his special movie clapperboard.

"Quiet, please," he began. "Lights, camera . . ."

The girls waited to hear the word "action", but nothing happened.

"The clapperboard is stuck," he said, frowning.

The flustered crew tried to get it working, but it refused to snap shut. An assistant ran up and passed the director two thick wooden sticks he had found in the props department.

"My camera won't work, either," said a confused camera operator.

"There's something funny going on around here," whispered Rachel.

"Look," Kirsty said quietly to her friend, pointing. "That camera's glowing!"

The girls stared as Keira whooshed out of the lens. "Oh girls," she cried. "Jack Frost has stolen my enchanted clapperboard, and given it to his goblins!"

Rachel and Kirsty were horrified. "What does it do?" asked Rachel.

"It makes sure filming always goes to plan," Keira explained.

"That must be why it's going wrong today," guessed Kirsty.

Suddenly there was a giggle outside the door, and the sound of footsteps on the stairs.

"That sounded like a goblin," said Kirsty. "Do you think the enchanted clapperboard is here?"

"If you were fairies," said Keira, "it would be much easier to search around without being seen."

Keira waved her wand and a cascade of golden fairy dust magically shrank them to fairy size.

"Let's go!" said Kirsty,

swooping upstairs and following the sound of
giggling into Mrs Croft's bedroom. Two goblins
were bouncing up and down on the bed. One
had a clapperboard under his arm.

"That's the enchanted clapperboard!" said Keira.

"Give that back to Keira right now!" declared
Rachel, fluttering forward.

The goblin was so surprised, he lost his balance
and bounced off the bed with a loud crash. Then,
without looking back, they both shot
out of the door, still clutching
the enchanted clapperboard.
At the top of the stairs,
the goblins were playing
tug-of-war with it, until
suddenly one of them
lost their balance,

and they both tumbled all the way down to the bottom of the steps.

"Come on!" Keira cried, zooming after the goblins. "We have to stop them!"

Downstairs, a sound technician had wedged her microphone in the old ceiling beams and three runners were trying to pull it free.

Half the costumes had gone missing, and the make-up artist's brushes had fallen through the floorboards. The poor director was sitting in the middle of it all with his head in his hands.

"We have to finish filming tonight," he muttered. "Mrs Croft is coming back tomorrow! Let's set up a screen and watch the rushes," he went on.

"What are the rushes?" asked Rachel as everyone sprang into action.

"They're the scenes from the day before,"

Keira explained. "The director always checks them to make sure they are fine."

The girls watched as two runners pointed a projector at the wall,

drew the curtains and turned off the lights. The
room was soon packed as everyone gathered for
the viewing.

Through the gloom, Kirsty saw something
move behind the sofa.

The goblins were watching the film scenes and
scowling. "I'd make a much better star," one said,
tucking the enchanted clapperboard under his
arm and jumping in front of the projector screen.

"No you wouldn't," squeaked the other one.
"*I* would!"

Everyone in the room gasped.

"Quick – grab it!" cried Keira.

The three fluttering fairies reached the
enchanted clapperboard a second too late.

"I don't remember filming this," said
the director in a puzzled voice, frowning.

The goblins began pushing each other as the outlines of their bodies filled the white wall behind them.

"Who hired these naughty extras?" he demanded. "And where did they get those hideous costumes?"

As the goblins shoved and fought, the enchanted clapperboard fell to the ground.

"This is our chance!" said Rachel. As a runner jumped up to chase the goblins from the room, the fairies zipped towards the clapperboard.

The film crew were so busy staring at the goblins, no one saw Keira land beside the clapperboard and shrink it back to fairy size.

"I've got it!" she cried, as the three of them swooped out through the open window.

Just then, they heard Mrs Croft's front door open, and the goblins ran out scowling, and disappeared into the woods.

"Thanks for your help today," said Keira. "Now filming can get back to normal."

With a swoop of her magic wand, she returned Kirsty and Rachel to their normal size.

"I'm going to take the enchanted clapperboard back to Fairyland," explained Keira. "But I've got a feeling that *The Starlight Chronicles* is going to be a sparkling success!"

With that, she disappeared in a burst of golden light. "We're ready for you, girls!" a runner called to them. "The cameras are working again."

Kirsty and Rachel hurried inside, just in time to hear the director say three truly magical words:

"Lights! Camera! Action!"

Holly the Christmas Fairy

Hillfields Farm

Christmas
Trees

HILLFIELDS
FARM

Tippington
Town

Santa's
Cabin

Rachel's
House

Shopping Centre

Three Days Until Christmas

It was the Christmas holidays and best friends
Rachel Walker and Kirsty Tate were at Rachel's
house in Tippington Town.

"Only three days to go until Christmas!"
smiled Kirsty, playing with her golden locket.
Both girls wore magical lockets. They had been
a present from their very special friends, the
Rainbow Magic fairies!

Mrs Walker came into the room. "Hello, girls! We're going to choose a Christmas tree later. Do you want to fetch the decorations from the garage?"

The girls ran to get the decorations. But as Rachel reached up for a box her locket burst open, scattering fairy dust everywhere!

"Kirsty!" Rachel cried as both girls began to grow small. "We're on our way to Fairyland!"

When the girls landed by the Fairyland Palace a few moments later, Queen Titania came towards them. "Our magic made your locket open,"

311

she said. "I'm afraid we need your help again!"

A pretty little fairy came towards the girls. She had long dark hair and wore a red dress with a furry hood. "Hello," she said sadly. "I'm Holly the Christmas Fairy. It's my job to make sure that Christmas is as sparkly and happy as possible."

"But Jack Frost is causing trouble," sighed Queen Titania. "We'll show you what happened." She waved her wand over a pool of water. Pictures began to appear on the surface.

Kirsty and Rachel saw a large log cabin,

surrounded by deep snow. Outside was a
beautiful sleigh, sparkling with magic.

"That's Santa's workshop, and his sleigh!"
Holly whispered to the girls.

Eight reindeer were harnessed to the sleigh.
Lots of elves were filling it with presents. But
then the spiky figure of Jack Frost appeared!

Jack Frost ran over to the sleigh and jumped
in. It lifted off the ground and zoomed away,

into the starry night sky. The picture in the pool faded away.

"We must find Santa's sleigh, or Christmas will be ruined," said the queen. "Plus there were three very special presents on the sleigh."

"We'll find the sleigh and the presents," the girls cried.

The queen gave the girls a little bag. Inside was a golden crown. "If you put this crown on Jack Frost's head, he will be brought back to Fairyland. Now, it's time for you to go home. Holly will come and see you soon!"

The queen sent a shower of shimmering fairy dust over both of the girls.

The two best friends smiled at each other. They were about to start another magical adventure!

That evening, the girls and Mr and Mrs Walker went to a farm to choose the Christmas tree. Buttons the dog came too!

Rachel soon spotted a beautiful tree.

Holly appeared in the branches!

Just then there was a shout from Mrs Walker, and Buttons dashed past the girls, barking loudly.

"Stop him, girls!" cried Mrs Walker.

"We'll catch him!" Rachel called.

Holly fluttered into Kirsty's pocket and the girls ran after Buttons. He was racing towards an old barn. Kirsty spotted a shadow in front of them with a pointed nose and big feet. It rushed into the barn.

"Oh!" she gasped, "I think Buttons is chasing one of Jack Frost's goblins!"

Rachel tied Buttons up outside the barn and the girls peeped inside. There were large open doors at the opposite end of the barn. A sparkling trail led out of the barn and right up into the sky. At the far end of the trail, they spotted Santa's sleigh disappearing into the distance!

"We've just missed Jack Frost," said Kirsty, looking disappointed.

Rachel noticed that the barn had wrapping paper scattered everywhere. "Mean Jack Frost has been opening Santa's presents!" she said crossly.

Just then the girls spotted two goblins.

They were squabbling over a super-sparkly present. "Look!" cried Kirsty. "It must be one of the three special presents the queen asked us to get."

"The other two presents must still be on the sleigh," Holly said.

"How are we going to get the present?" Rachel whispered.

Kirsty thought hard. "I've got an idea," she said to the others. "Holly, could you magic up the smell of mince pies?"

Holly's eyes twinkled. "Of course," she replied.

"We'll tell the greedy goblins there's a big plate of mince pies in the hayloft," Kirsty went on. "They'll have to put the present down to climb into the hayloft and then we'll be able to grab the present!"

"Great idea!" said Holly. "One magic smell of hot mince pies coming up!" And she flew towards the goblins.

Rachel and Kirsty watched anxiously as Holly fluttered over the goblins' heads. Would their plan work…? Holly waved her wand. Moments later the smell of mince pies drifted around the barn.

The goblins sniffed curiously.

"Fresh mince pies, up in the hayloft!" Holly called. "Help yourselves."

"Mince pies! Yum!" shouted the goblins. They threw the present down on a pile of straw and scrambled up the ladder.

When they had reached the top, the girls dashed quickly into the barn and Kirsty picked up the parcel.

Suddenly there was a shout from the goblins. "There aren't any mince pies here! We've been tricked!"

"Quick!" gasped Holly, "let's get out of here!"

The girls and Holly ran to the door as the goblins tumbled down the ladder.

Outside the barn Rachel untied Buttons. The goblins appeared in the doorway and ran towards her. But Buttons began to bark loudly and the two terrified creatures shot back into the barn and slammed the door.

"Good dog!" said Rachel, patting Buttons.

"Hurrah! We've found one special present," Holly beamed. "Thank you so much!"

"We'll see you again soon," Rachel called, as Holly flew up into the sky.

"I'll be back as soon as I find out where Jack Frost is now!" Holly promised.

Rachel and Kirsty hurried back to the farm. Rachel's mum and dad were tying the Christmas tree to the roof of the car.

"Let's head home for mince pies and hot chocolate," said Rachel's mum, and they all climbed into the car.

Rachel and Kirsty grinned at each other.

"I think Buttons deserves a mince pie too," Kirsty whispered. "After all, he was the one who led us to the goblins and the first present."

"Woof!" Buttons agreed.

"Yes, and our fairy adventures aren't over yet," Rachel said, her eyes shining. "We still have to save the sleigh and find two presents!"

Search for the Sleigh

The next morning the girls were getting ready to go Christmas shopping with Rachel's mum.

"I hope we can find Jack Frost and Santa's sleigh today," said Kirsty.

Rachel nodded. "Yes. Then we can really start to enjoy Christmas!"

The girls clattered downstairs together.

Mrs Walker was waiting for them in the hall.

"Don't forget your scarves and gloves," she said. "It's freezing today!" She opened the front door and went to get the car from the garage.

"Doesn't the tree look fantastic?" said Kirsty, looking at the glittering tree in the hall.

Looking closely, Rachel noticed that there was a beautiful fairy at the top of the tree. It was Holly the Christmas Fairy!

Holly flew down onto Kirsty's shoulder. "Hello, girls!" she said in her tinkly voice. "I think something magical is going to happen today,

so can I come to the shops with you?"

"Of course," Rachel
replied happily. She
ran upstairs to fetch
the bag containing
the golden crown,
given to them by
Queen Titania. If
they could put it on Jack
Frost's head, he would be

instantly returned to Fairyland to face the
king and queen!

Holly fluttered into Kirsty's coat pocket.

When they reached the shopping centre,
Mrs Walker arranged to meet the girls by the
lifts an hour later. Then she went to buy some
last-minute gifts.

The girls really enjoyed seeing the Christmas displays in the shops. Holly was peeping out from Kirsty's pocket to see what was going on. She was so tiny that nobody spotted her!

In the central square of the shopping centre was Santa's Grotto. It was a white tent covered in sparkling lights and surrounded by fake snow.

Rachel and Kirsty saw a little girl run out of the grotto to join her mum. "Santa wasn't nice!"

she cried. "And he was all cold and spiky!"

Immediately Rachel's ears pricked up. That didn't sound like Santa at all. But it did sound like someone else they knew… Jack Frost!

"Kirsty!" Rachel said worriedly, pulling her friend close. "I think Jack Frost is inside the grotto, pretending to be Santa!"

"Let's check it out!" Holly piped up from inside Kirsty's pocket. "But how will we get in?"

"We'll slip in round the back and see what's going on," said Kirsty.

The girls tiptoed round to the back of the grotto. Lifting up the tent they crept inside and hid behind a cluster of rocks.

Gleaming icicles hung from the high ceiling,

and a big Christmas tree stood in one corner.

And there, wearing a santa suit, was Jack
Frost! He was sitting in Santa's sparkling sleigh.
The sleigh was still loaded with presents.

"Bring me another present!" Jack Frost roared.

His goblin servants rushed towards him and
pushed more presents into Jack Frost's greedy hands.

Suddenly Kirsty spotted something. "Look!"
she hissed. "It's one of the special presents!" The
shiny parcel was sitting at the back of the sleigh.

"You're right," Holly whispered excitedly.

"But how are we going to get hold of the present without being spotted?" Rachel asked.

"I can distract Jack Frost," said Holly with a smile. "I'll use my magic to hide inside one of the presents he is opening."

"Good idea!" Rachel declared. "We'll creep up to the back of the sleigh and grab the present."

"And we'll try to put the special crown on Jack Frost's head," Kirsty whispered. "Let's go!"

They began to crawl towards the sleigh.

Soon the special present was so close that Kirsty could reach out and touch it!

"Now we just wait for Holly to appear," Rachel whispered, moving closer to Jack Frost so she could put the magic crown on his head.

Jack Frost ripped the paper off another parcel and held up a wooden box. "I wonder what's in here?" he muttered.

Suddenly the lid of the box burst open. Holly shot out in a shower of glittering red fairy dust!

Jack Frost and his goblins stared at Holly in stunned surprise. Kirsty stretched out her hands and grabbed the special parcel.

"Grab that pesky Christmas Fairy!" Jack Frost shouted furiously.

Goblins in the Grotto!

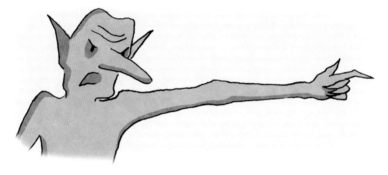

Just then, one of the goblins spotted Rachel and Kirsty. "Look out!" he screeched.

Jack Frost quickly waved his wand and the reindeer all instantly galloped off, pulling the sleigh behind them.

"Grab that fairy and the interfering girls!" Jack Frost roared at his goblin servants.

"Kirsty! Rachel!" shouted Holly, who was zooming up and away from the goblins. "You've got to get out of here!"

The reindeer galloped out of the tent and flew up into the air. As the sleigh soared out of the shopping centre, the shoppers looked up in amazement. They began cheering, thinking it was some sort of fabulous Christmas magic show!

Meanwhile, the goblins were closing in on the girls, and Rachel and Kirsty ran away from them. The goblins chased them, but they kept tripping over their big feet!

The girls rushed out of the grotto. "Quick, Kirsty!" Rachel shouted. "Pull on the support ropes at the back of the tent!"

The two girls began pulling at the ropes with all their might. Suddenly there was a creaking sound.

The large tent wobbled and then fell to the ground, trapping the goblins underneath the canvas!

"We did it!" Kirsty cheered.

Holly zoomed over to land on Kirsty's shoulder. "Thank you for getting the second present," she smiled.

"It's such a shame Jack Frost got away again," sighed Rachel. "And we don't know where he's gone."

"Oh, yes, we do!"
Holly told her excitedly.
"I followed the sleigh
and spoke to one of
the reindeers. He told
me that they are taking
Jack Frost to his Ice
Castle."

The girls shivered.
They knew that the Ice
Castle was a cold and scary place!

Holly smiled at them. "I'll take this second
present back to Fairyland now. Tomorrow
we'll find the final present and get Santa's
sleigh back!" The little fairy blew kisses to the
girls and disappeared. The girls went to the lifts
to meet Mrs Walker.

Rachel's mum was already waiting for them and they all headed off to the car. The girls clutched each other's hands. They felt very excited and a little bit nervous about visiting the Ice Castle the next day!

Rachel woke up early the next morning with a yawn. Then she remembered.

"It's Christmas Eve!" she cried excitedly. She went across to the window and saw that the garden was covered with sparkling white snow!

Kirsty woke up and the two best friends peered out of the window.

"I can't wait for Christmas," Rachel smiled.

"I know," Kirsty agreed. "We just have to find Father Christmas's sleigh and the last present!"

The two girls threw on their clothes and hurried downstairs for breakfast. Then they pulled on their coats and boots and ran out into the garden.

The girls had fun throwing snowballs at each other. But one exploded in the air, and Holly appeared!

"Are you ready, girls?" she cried. "It's time to go to Jack Frost's Ice Castle!"

"We're ready!" Rachel said bravely. The girls knew that time would stand still in the human world whilst they were away. Kirsty nodded, making sure that she had the bag containing the special crown.

Holly waved her magic wand in the air and moments later the girls found themselves sitting in a tree, staring up at Jack Frost's Ice Castle.

The castle was built from sheets of ice. It looked cold and scary!

The three friends flew off in different directions to look for a way in to the castle.

After a few minutes of searching, clever Holly found a trapdoor and used her magic to open the heavy door.

"Let's search for Santa's sleigh," Rachel whispered.

The friends flew down the winding staircase towards the ground floor of the castle. But they bumped straight into lots of goblin guards. The three of them were captured!

The goblins laughed gleefully. "We're going to take you to Jack Frost!" they gloated.

The goblins led the three fairies through the Ice Castle and into the Great Hall. There was Jack Frost, sitting in Santa's sleigh! The reindeer were still harnessed to it, munching on bales of hay.

Jack Frost looked up at the girls. "You again!" he snarled nastily.

Rachel gasped as she saw the present that Jack Frost was holding. It was the third special present that the queen had asked the girls to find!

Rachel could see that Holly and Kirsty had spotted the present too. But how could they stop Jack Frost from opening it…?

Suddenly, Kirsty gasped. She had an idea.

"Rachel," she whispered. "Can you distract the goblins and Jack Frost?"

Rachel nodded. She flapped her gossamer wings furiously and the goblin holding her loosened his grip. Rachel zoomed up into the air!

"Seize her!" Jack Frost yelled in anger.

The goblins rushed after Rachel, trying to grab her and pull her back down.

Meanwhile, Kirsty grabbed a piece of silver wrapping paper and a purple ribbon from the floor. She took the bag with the magic crown

in it out of her pocket and quickly wrapped it up.

Jack Frost waved his wand, and instantly Rachel's wings froze in mid-air. She fell to the

ground, landing on top of two goblins. Luckily, somehow she wasn't hurt!

"Now!" said Jack, "I'm opening this present!"

"Please, Your Majesty," said Kirsty, stepping forward. "We only came to get this one very special present." And she held up the crown, wrapped in silver paper. "It's for the Fairy King. We have to take it to him!"

Jack Frost's eyes lit up as he stared at the parcel. "A present for King Oberon?" he muttered. "It will be mine!"

Jack Frost snatched it right out of her hands.

Kirsty tried not to smile. She knew greedy Jack Frost wouldn't be able to resist taking the present for himself! He pulled off the ribbon, and

tore the paper away to reveal the bag. He put his hand inside and drew out the glittering crown.

"Aha!" he declared triumphantly. "A sparkling new crown, just for me!" And he put the crown on his head.

Immediately, Jack Frost vanished!

"Jack Frost's been sent straight to the king and queen," cried Rachel in delight. She jumped into the magic sleigh and picked up the third present. "Let's get out of this icy place!"

Holly patted one of the reindeer on the head.
"Take us back to Santa, please!"

The reindeer began to gallop down the
Great Hall. Goblins jumped out of the way as
the sleigh picked up speed. Then it rose into the
air, magically passing through the roof of the
castle and up into the clouds.

After a few minutes, the girls saw the pretty

log cabin that they
had first seen in the
fairy pool. The sleigh
landed and a big
group of cheering
elves ran over to it.

Rachel and Kirsty
gasped with delight
as they saw Santa,

dashing out of the cabin.

"Are we in time to save Christmas, Santa?" Rachel asked him anxiously.

Santa nodded. "Oh, yes," he smiled. "It's going to be a wonderful Christmas, thanks to you!"

"Now," said Santa, "The king and queen will want to see you. Come with me and I'll drop you off on my way to deliver these gifts."

Rachel and Kirsty couldn't believe it. They were going to ride with Santa Claus in his sleigh, on Christmas Eve!

As the sleigh drew closer to Fairyland, there was a shout of welcome from the fairies below.

Rachel and Kirsty waved as they saw all their old friends waiting for them.

"We brought you this," Rachel said, stepping out of the sleigh and handing the third special present to King Oberon.

Santa waved as his sleigh soared off into the sky. He had a lot of work to do!

"What's happened to Jack Frost?" asked Rachel.

The king looked stern. "He has had his magic powers taken away from him for a whole year," he explained seriously.

The queen nodded. "But now it's time to celebrate Christmas, and we have special gifts for the three of you."

The girls gasped in surprise as the queen gave them the two special presents they had rescued from Jack Frost! The king handed Holly the parcel that Rachel had just given him.

There was a new wand for Holly, and when she waved it the sweet sound of tinkling Christmas bells could be heard.

Rachel and Kirsty's presents both contained beautiful fairy dolls!

"These are fairies for the top of your Christmas trees," the queen explained.

Rachel and Kirsty were thrilled to bits.

"But now it's time for you to go home to enjoy Christmas!" the king said.

The girls quickly said their goodbyes.

"Merry Christmas!" called all the fairies as the girls were whizzed away in a haze of magical sparkles. Soon Rachel and Kirsty found themselves back in the Walkers' garden.

"We did it, Rachel!" Kirsty laughed happily.

"We saved Christmas!"

The girls ran inside and put Rachel's fairy doll carefully on the top of the tree. Just then the doorbell rang. It was Kirsty's mum and dad!

"Merry Christmas!" said Mr and Mrs Tate with a smile, rushing to hug Kirsty.

Soon it was time for Kirsty to go home for Christmas. She gave Rachel a huge hug.

"I just know we're going to have the best Christmas ever!" Kirsty whispered.

"I know," Rachel smiled. "And I can't wait to have more magical adventures with my best friend and our special fairy friends!"

RAINBOW magic™

Become a
Rainbow Magic
fairy friend and be the first to
see sneak peeks of new books.

There are lots of special offers and exclusive
competitions to win sparkly
Rainbow Magic prizes.

Sign up today at
www.rainbowmagicbooks.co.uk